On the Cutting Edge
Resolution

By J.J. Luepke
© 2012

Order this book online at www.trafford.com
or email orders@trafford.com

Most Trafford titles are also available at major online book retailers.

Printed in the United States of America.

ISBN: 978-1-4669-7089-2 (sc)
ISBN: 978-1-4669-7090-8 (e)

Library of Congress Control Number: 2012922763

Trafford rev. 12/10/2012

 www.trafford.com

North America & international
toll-free: 1 888 232 4444 (USA & Canada)
phone: 250 383 6864 ♦ fax: 812 355 4082

Dedication

This book is dedicated to all the would-be Josie Buchannans in the world who long to keep their dream job and find Mr. Right with whom they can share their lives. I also want to thank all my friends and relatives who helped me get this book to press in spite of holidays, illnesses, and accidents. You are extremely instrumental in the success of this novel. Thank you!

Chapter One
New Year's Eve

Josephine 'Josie' Buchannon felt like the luckiest, most blessed woman alive on New Year's Eve. She was wearing a fabulous sapphire blue evening gown with rhinestone trim, seated at a corner booth in the most elegant restaurant in Lakewood, NY with her fiancé P.J. Coleson, formerly of New York City.

"How do you like the sapphire and diamond necklace I gave you as a belated Christmas present, Josie?" P.J. asked, looking quite dapper in his black satin tuxedo. The candlelight sparkled in their love-struck eyes. It flickered in time with the sultry background music. The atmosphere was intoxicating, is what Josie was thinking.

"It is the most exquisite thing I've ever seen," Josie said, fingering the delicate pendant. "Are you sure you like the sapphire and diamond men's engagement ring I gave you?" She looked at him.

"Yes, honey. It's great!" P.J. cupped Josie's face in his hands and kissed her long and hard. Josie sighed. She felt like she was floating on air. The waiter came with their beverage order, an O 'Doul's for P.J. and a lemon water for Josie. He set them gently on the table and asked if they were ready to order.

"I'll have your prime rib special," P.J. answered. "How about you, honey? What'll you have?"

"That sounds good," Josie said, not having looked at the menu. "Make mine the same, please."

"How would you like them done?" The waiter asked. Josie shrugged. She was more into her date than her plate.

"Medium-well," she said without looking away from P.J. "Thanks."

"I'll have medium-rare, please," P.J. said. Hold the potatoes, fat free French dressing on the salads, and no dessert. Thanks!'"

"How about using this time to discuss some wedding plans?" P.J. asked.

"I didn't bring my wedding planner along," Josie said and sat up straight. She had purchased a special book that gave her ideas, tips and guidance on every nuance of wedding planning. It even had pockets in which she could store dress material samples, catalog cutouts and stationery samples. It seemed to be quite thorough. There were so many ideas offered in that guide Josie could not imagine using them all. Some were just too extensive; others, too complicated. She might be rich now, by some standards, but she was still frugal. Her late father would not want her to waste his money on fluffy nonsense, she highly suspected.

Not for the first time, she wished her father had come forward to claim his relationship with her before his lover, Cassandra Coven, murdered him. Coven was the former manager of Sanderson & Sons Advertising Agency and Josie's immediate supervisor. She now had a permanent address in solitary confinement at the women's penitentiary, or so Josie hoped, and Josie was running the firm as Lew Sanderson's rightful owner.

"So, sweetie, what did you want to talk about concerning the wedding?" Josie asked, turning her attention to happier thoughts.

"Like, who walks with whom? How do you pick that— by how close we are to them as friend, or by height, or what?" P.J.'s brow furrowed. Josie smiled.

"Of course, the maid of honor walks with the best man. After that, it usually makes better pictures to pair them up by height. We will take your two shortest friends and pair them with your sisters. The Schneider brothers are both tall, so it really doesn't matter. Did you have a preference?"

"No, but they do," P.J. said and wiggled his eyebrows.

Josie chuckled and said, "I bet they do. So, what are they?"

"The guys saw your staff Christmas photo from your holiday ad. Pete has a girlfriend, so he's okay with walking with Jessica since she's already married. Dave, on the other hand, would very much like to meet Donna. I told him about her punk-Goth period, and he's intrigued." He wiggled his eyebrows again and grinned."

"Oh, you men! You are interested in the weirdest things sometimes!" Josie playfully slapped P.J.'s shoulder.

At that point, the waiter returned with their salads, and they began eating their supper. The steaks arrived not long after that, and soon it was time to leave for the New Year's Eve Ball.

The city council had hired a live band for the ball that was being held at the Lakewood Community Center, just a couple of blocks east of Sanderson & Sons, along Main Street. The orchestra from the community college played Gershwin waltzes and some pops songs. Josie remembered her grandmother listening to that kind of music when she was younger. She still had some old Long Playing Albums she kept in the sitting room.

P.J. twirled Josie around the floor under the disco ball. Some people may think that the disco ball should have been outlawed when disco dancing died away, but Josie liked it. The shards of glass reflected the colored stage lights all over the ceiling, the walls, and the dancers. It was romantic.

Halfway through the evening, workers in black slacks and white tops passed out party favors. Their boxes contained all sorts of New Year's Eve hats, noisemakers, plastic leis and streamers. P.J. picked through the box until he found the last crown and placed it on Josie's head. He picked a bowler derby for himself and a couple of streamers. He handed one of the streamers to Josie.

"Aren't you sweet," Josie murmured in P.J.'s ear as he took her in his arms for a slow dance. "You make me feel like the homecoming queen."

"That's what I was going for, babe."

Suddenly, the music stopped. The bandleader stood up and pulled a microphone off its stand to make an announcement.

"We have just one minute to midnight. Everyone get with the partner you want to be with to ring in the New Year. We want to thank the City of Lakewood for inviting us to share this festive evening with you. Be sure to call 1-WE

DRIVE YOU if you've had too much to drink. They'll get you home safely. Everyone in their places? Let's start the ten second countdown . . . now! Ten, nine, eight, seven, six, five, four, three, two, one!

"Happy New Year!" everyone shouted with him. Then P.J., like most of the other men in the hall, took his sweetheart into his arms and gave her that once-a-year kiss. He dipped her low for a few moments and then pulled her up without breaking contact until they were upright again.

"P.J.! Now, I'm dizzy with the blood rushing to my head as well as from kissing you!"

"Happy New Year, Josie, and many more," P.J. said softly, gazing into her eyes.

"Happy New Year, P.J. I love you," she replied.

"Do you know that the person you're with at midnight New Year's Eve is the person you'll spend the entire next year with?" P.J. asked, guiding her off the dance floor and to an empty table.

"I should hope so!" Josie answered, setting her tiny evening bag on the tabletop.

"Would you care for a drink?" P.J. asked. She nodded and watched him weave his way to the bar. Then she glanced around the room to see if she could spot anyone she knew. Before she had spanned the entire place, Donna Schmidt and her date d'jour plopped themselves onto the extra chairs at Josie's table. Donna was wearing a rag-hemmed gauze gown with a peasant top and lace-up boots. Her date was wearing a tuxedo printed t-shirt, black jeans and high top tennis shoes.

"Hi, Boss! Nice dance, huh?" Donna asked. Josie smiled and nodded. "Hey, I want you to meet Terry Richards, here. He's in town just for the weekend. We used to go to school together."

"Hello, Terry," Josie said. "What field are you in?"

"Oh, I'm not a farmer, Ma'am," Terry said, shaking his shaggy black hair. "I'm into race cars and work as a pit crewman for a Busch Series racer who likes to travel. I'm just home for the holidays. Nice to meet you. Come on, Donna, let's dance!" Donna shrugged her shoulders, waved goodbye to Josie, and followed her date onto the dance floor.

Just then, P.J. returned with a couple of Diet Cokes and set them on the table. He took a seat next to her and took a swig of his soda pop. "Wasn't that Donna from work?"

"Yes, and her date, Terry Richards. Apparently, he works for a traveling race car driver, so they're home for the holidays." Josie took a sip of her drink as well. "For a second there, I thought he looked familiar."

"Fascinating," P.J. said. "Did you want to dance some more, or are you ready to leave?"

"Let's blow this gin joint!" Josie said, and then giggled. "I've always wanted to say that, but never had the opportunity." P.J. laughed with her. He stood up, took her hand and led her to the coat check stand to collect her cape. Along the way, he drew out his car keys and hit the sequence that would start the engine automatically. It would take the chill off the interior by the time they reached it.

P.J. took Josie back to his apartment. They had spent a handful of nights cuddled on his couch when she had to take care of him after he had burned his hands in a work-related accident. They would fall asleep watching a movie or one of their favorite detective shows on TV. He had rented a romantic movie for tonight, not knowing what to expect. It was New Year's Eve, and they were engaged to be married. The wedding was set for the first Saturday in April. That seemed so far off. He hung up her cape and his tux jacket in the hall closet and returned to the living room.

"Would you like a glass of wine to toast the New Year?" he asked Josie, raising his eyebrows. He knew she didn't routinely drink alcoholic beverages, but this was a special occasion. And, it wasn't like he was offering her hard liquor.

"Okay, sure," she said, surprising him. He nearly tripped over his own two feet on the way to the refrigerator. He set a bottle of Blue Nun on the countertop and reached into the upper cabinet for wine glasses. He had purchased a matched pair the other day in preparation for tonight. After filling the glasses halfway, he put the bottle back into the refrigerator. Josie toyed with the idea of getting drunk tonight. A lot of people drink to excess on New Year's Eve, she rationalized. *And, I'm not going to be driving home.*

"I'm sorry it's not an expensive brand of wine," he said as he handed one of the glasses to Josie, "but, I wasn't sure you would drink any of it, and I didn't want it to go to waste."

Josie held up her glass for the toast and looked at P.J. expectantly.

"Right, here goes. To a New Year filled with love and passion, to a smooth wedding and the best honeymoon anyone could ever wish for!" P.J. said, and clinked glasses with her. Then they both took a sip of wine.

"Here's to success and prosperity in all we do, and may we do it all together," Josie said. They clinked glasses and took another drink. She set her goblet on the end table, smoothed her dress and took a seat on the couch. "What movie did you rent?"

P.J. set his glass next to hers and stepped over to the television, picked up the plastic case laying there and looked for the title, "It's 'old school'. I hope you don't mind. Tell me if you've seen it already. I can pull out something else. It's *Dirty Dancing*, with Patrick Swayze and Jennifer Gray."

"Would you believe that I have never seen it, but others have told me that it is a lot more romantic than the title would lead you to believe." She picked up her glass of wine and took a sip. P.J. smiled at her and inserted the DVD. Then, he went to sit by her on the couch. He reached across her to pick up his wine glass, kissing her neck as he did so. Not watching what he was doing, he caught the base of the stemware on the lip of the end table and spilled it down the front of Josie's evening gown. Josie gasped.

"Ooh! That's going to stain," P.J. said lamely. "I'm really sorry. I'll pay for the dry cleaning." He got up and ran to the kitchen for a towel. He grabbed the whole roll of paper towels from the counter top and ran back to the living room, unrolling sheet after sheet as he went. He handed the bundle to Josie who sopped up as much as she could get.

"P.J., could I borrow a pair of your pajamas so I can treat this dress before the stain sets? Would you have some club soda in the refrigerator? I can treat the stain with that. It should help." She got up and headed down the hall toward P.J.'s bedroom. She had been in his bedroom only once; the day she helped him move in. She had carefully avoided that end of the apartment ever since.

"Uh, yeah," P.J. said, tossing roll of paper towels toward the counter on his way back to the bedroom. He rummaged through the chest of drawers and brought out a brand new package. "I sleep in my boxers," he said, and blushed. "My parents are always giving me presents I never use."

"Thanks," Josie said, shifting the paper towel to one hand and taking the new pajamas in the other. "Please unzip my dress for me, and then set out that club soda. I'll be out in a jiffy."

"Okay!" P.J. said, waiting for her to turn around. He reached up with trembling hands and slid down the zipper head. Just as he thought, she didn't have on a bra. His breath caught in his throat and his pulse began to race.

"Please get out that club soda, now," Josie said, clutching her dress to her as she turned back to face him.

"Uh huh," he mumbled, spinning around before he lost control of himself.

"Shut the door behind you," she said and watched him leave, doing as she had told him. Dropping the dress quickly, she tore into the pajama package, plastic wrap flying in all directions. She snapped out each piece and slid into them, having to roll over the waistline several times. Then she cuffed the bottoms and the sleeves. Once she was satisfied the pants weren't going to fall off with her first few steps, she picked up her dress off the floor and headed back to the kitchen. P.J. had left out the club soda, as she had asked, so she was able to hold the dress over the kitchen sink and apply the stain removing beverage. She rubbed the skirt against the bodice, hoping it would not wreck the material. Then, she squeezed out as much soda as she could and went to hang up the dress in the hall closet.

Returning to the living room, Josie sat down next to P.J. and picked up her wine glass. She downed what was left and made a face. "It got warm. Eew. But I have thought of another toast. P.J., may I have some more wine, please?"

P.J. trotted to the kitchen to fetch the Blue Nun and quickly returned. He refilled both their glasses. They held them up for the toast.

"Here's to a year with no murders!" They clinked their glasses and then drained them. P.J. took both goblets and rinsed them in the sink while asking, "Would you like to watch the movie in my room? I've got a small flat screen TV that has a built-in DVD player. It will be more comfortable than sleeping double on the couch again."

"That is probably true. Let's test that theory," Josie said, surprising herself. Then, she let out a burp. "Oops! Excuse me!" Then, she giggled. P.J. was by her side in a heartbeat.

"Are you okay?" he asked, taking her by the elbow.

"Mm hmm," she murmured and leaned against him. P.J. put one arm around her and reached out with the other for the DVD. Then, he guided Josie down the hall to his bedroom. He set the video on the chest near the TV and turned to help Josie get into bed. He pulled down the navy blue comforter and matching sheet. Then, he swooped Josie off her feet and laid her on the mattress. She slid in further and pulled up the covers while P.J. went to the TV and inserted the DVD, pressing "Play" on the remote. He adjusted the volume before putting the remote on the nightstand. Next, P.J. slipped out of his tuxedo pants and white shirt, sat down on the bed and removed his socks. Rolling into bed and drawing the covers up in one smooth motion, he turned toward Josie.

"I want you," he whispered in her ear." He rolled toward Josie, leaned down and kissed her neck.

"I wuv you, too," she mumbled and rolled away from him with her eyes closed.

"I don't think you heard me, dear," P.J. spoke a little above a whisper this time. "I want you. I don't know if I can wait until our wedding night to make love to you . . . Josie?" He touched her shoulder and leaned over to look into her face. She started snoring softly.

"Good thing this *isn't* our wedding night," P.J. said to himself. "That would be disastrous. As it is, it's probably the best thing that could happen to us. Lord, you've got some sense of humor. I should have known better. I'm sorry." He shook his head, picked up his pillow and went to sleep in the living room thinking it would serve as penance for what he had been hoping to do with Josie that night.

Chapter Two
New Year's Day

Josie woke the next morning with a fuzzy head. She looked around P.J.'s bedroom and wondered for just a moment how she had gotten there, and why she was alone.

"Oh, yeah," she mumbled. It was New Year's Eve last night. They'd both a had a little wine, and so had her dress. She made a face. Pulling her tongue off the roof of her mouth, she crawled out of bed. Looking down, she noted she was wearing a pair of blue paisley print pajamas that were a mile too big on her. *Oh, yeah, P.J. lent them to me*, she remembered. She padded down the hallway to the bathroom and used the extra toothbrush to clean the cotton feeling from her mouth.

The running water must have awakened P.J. because he came sloughing into the bathroom, too.

"Good morning, sleepyhead," he said and put his arms around her from the back. They both looked in the mirror and rolled their eyes. Their hair stood on end and black circles haunted their eyes.

"Good morning, yourself!" she responded, then stuck the filled toothbrush in her mouth. She slid over so he could fill his own brush and take care of morning breath, too.

"Care for some breakfast?" P.J. asked as he filled a spare glass with rinse water.

"Not. Really. Hungry," she answered between rinsings "How about we stop by Starbuck's on the way back to my place?"

"Sounds good. I can always get a breakfast burrito along the way, too. Do you think your dress is wearable this morning? Or, would you like a pair of my jogging pants and a t-shirt to wear home?"

"And, a sweatshirt," Josie added. "As you saw, I didn't wear a bra. Guess I didn't plan the evening out very well." She splashed some cold water on her face and patted it dry. "Thanks for having an extra toothbrush on hand, honey."

Once they were out in the brisk January air and on the road, Josie found her appetite again. They decided to stop at a Perkins for breakfast.

"I love their new French toast," Josie said. "It's fabulous."

"My favorite is the Magnificent Seven," P.J. said.

"How you can pack all that away, I'll never know," Josie responded. "By the way, we haven't selected a menu or a caterer yet. What kind of meat would you like for the wedding dinner?"

"Don't couples usually serve two kinds of meat?"

"That's probably because they can't agree on just one, or because the groom is such a pig!" Josie teased.

"Oink, oink."

"Seriously, you ham! What kind of meat do you want to eat at our wedding?"

"Pulled pork; how about that?"

"Just like a guy to want something messy. What happens to my white dress if I spill?"

"If you don't want any stains, you'd better not serve anything but water, or wear a bib. Anyway, isn't that why we pick two kinds of meat?" P.J. asked. "What's your favorite kind of meat?"

"I prefer chicken breast, of course. Without any barbeque sauce or anything, it's not as messy and won't stain my dress."

They finished their meal playfully and drove off to the handsome Victorian Drama style home that would someday be all theirs. Eleanor had given them the deed at Christmas, but she has the prerogative to live there until the wedding or until she moves into her new apartment. She told Josie she was having the owner paint it and put in new carpet before she moves a stick of furniture in there.

"Happy New Year!" Josie's grandmother, Eleanor, greeted the lovebirds. "I trust you slept well. Goodness, Josie, what happened to your dress? Let me see that."

"I accidently spilled wine on it last night," P.J. confessed. "I'm sorry. I'll pay for the dry cleaning."

"I used club soda on it right away, Grams. Just like you taught me," Josie said.

"Come into the kitchen and keep me company in the kitchen while I make some lunch."

"We just came from Perkins, Grams. I couldn't eat another bite for a couple of hours yet," Josie said, giving her grandmother a hug and a kiss on the cheek. "I'm going to shower; I'll be back in a jiffy."

Josie left for the stairs, and Eleanor led P.J. to the kitchen anyway, saying, "I've just put the kettle on. I'm sure you both have time for tea, at least, before you go on with your holiday. So, P.J., have a seat and tell me what the two of you plan to do today?"

Meanwhile, Josie was rummaging through her chest of drawers for her skinny jeans, her powder blue ski sweater and her wool socks. When they were piled on the bed, she shed P.J.'s sweats and hopped into the shower. She hummed a couple of refrains of the Hallelujah Chorus before rinsing the conditioner out of her hair. Then she toweled off and jumped into her clothes. She and P.J. had decided to go ice skating after she cleaned up. She blew her hair dry and applied a little mascara and lip gloss to finish the natural look she was accustomed to and headed for the stairs.

"Hi, honey!" P.J. greeted as she entered the kitchen. "Your grandmother has challenged us to a Rummy tournament with her and her friend, Nellie Pederson. What do you say, sweetie? Are you up to it?"

"Nellie will be here in half an hour," Eleanor interjected, "and she's bringing fresh apple pie and a bridge mix. Besides, the weatherman said it's not going to get over zero for a temperature today. I don't want you getting sick again like you did before Thanksgiving when you were dowsed by Bobbie's sprinkler system." Josie looked from Grams to P.J. and back again.

"Will you make your famous homemade hot chocolate?" Josie asked, raising her eyebrows.

"You know it!" Eleanor said with glee. "Great, I'll get right on it, so it will be ready when Nellie gets here. P.J. will you set up the card table and chairs, please? You know where they are in the closet, right?"

"Yes, Ma'am!" P.J. hopped out of his chair and headed down the hall to perform his chore.

"Josie, will you get out the party plates and matching cups, please? I'd really appreciate that."

"My pleasure, Grams," Josie said. "Getting to spend some more time with you before you move out is just what the doctor ordered." She walked over to the cabinet that was actually the back of the built-in china cabinet that faced the formal dining room. Opening a door on the bottom half, she counted out four of the rectangle, cut crystal plates and four matching cups. Each cup fit inside a ring on a plate so that they could be set on someone's lap, when seated on a chair or couch, without sliding off.

Ding dong, the front doorbell chimed. P.J. must have gotten the door as he came in carrying Nellie's pie and with Nellie on his heels.

"Hello, Eleanor!" Nellie greeted her friend with a hug. "Hello, Josie! How nice to see you! Oh, just set the pie on the stove for now, P.J. It has to cool off. Thank you! Then, take my coat and throw it on the couch or something, please. Thanks! It smells like hot chocolate in here! That will go nicely with this candy. Josie, be a dear and put these in a candy dish. Thanks!"

"Yes, Nellie! Good to see you too!" Josie accepted the bridge mix and went back to the china cabinet for a bowl. "How are you today? Did you and Grams stay up and watch the ball drop in New York on TV last night? I haven't had a chance to ask her yet."

"Oh, yes! We had the big wide-screen TV in the community room on all evening. It showed the ball drop at midnight, like usual. That new guy they have hosting the event just isn't the same as Dick Clark. I'm so sorry Mr. Clark passed away. Here, Josie, I'll take the bridge mix if you'll help your grandmother with the hot chocolate mugs." She took the bowl of candy from Josie and left the room. Eleanor picked up two cups by their handles, one in each hand, and followed Nellie. Josie followed suit.

Grams and Nellie are dressed a lot alike today, Josie thought. *I wonder if they shopped at the same store to get matching New Year's sweaters. They're a lot louder than Grams usually wears.*

P.J. had the table and chairs set up in the middle of the living room. The Buchannons seldom used the formal sitting room ever since Eleanor's best friend, Virginia Fieney, had been killed there. The women set down the treats on the card table, and Eleanor pulled four napkins from her slacks pocket.

"We'll cut the pie after we've played cards for an hour or two, okay?" Nellie asked. Everyone agreed. Eleanor stepped off to the side to fetch a deck of cards, notepaper and pen from a nearby cabinet, then returned to take her seat across from Nellie. If they played partners, the lovebirds could be on the same team.

"Before we begin," Nellie said, "I have an invitation for the two of you from all of us who play cards with your grandmother. We would like to throw the two of you a wedding shower next Sunday. Would 2 p.m. work for you? We'll have it at the community room of our apartment building."

Josie and P.J. looked at each other. P.J. shrugged and said, "I haven't got any plans. Have you, Josie?"

"No, I don't," she answered. "But, isn't that kind of early? Don't most people give them about a month before the wedding? Are you sure you have enough time to plan one?"

"Yes, dear," Eleanor said. "I've been privy to their planning sessions. They're ready."

"Your bridesmaids and groomsmen are invited, too, of course," Nellie added. "I know some probably won't be able to make it on this short notice, but that's life, and, life's the reason we're jumping on this so fast. At our age, you don't know if you'll be around next week, let alone three months from now. Even if we are, there's no guaranteeing we'll remember what we said three months prior. So, please indulge us. We're not getting any younger."

Josie and P.J. smiled at each other, first, then at Nellie and Eleanor.

"Yes, of course, we'll come," The bridal couple said in unison, accepting the invitation to attend a bridal shower at the Silver Seasons Apartments to be held the following Sunday.

"Great! You've made an old woman very happy." Then Nellie, being the visiting lady, dealt out the cards.

Chapter Three
Showers

The rest of the week was "nose to the grindstone" for Josie. She ended up taking work home with her every night. She and P.J. spent maybe ten minutes on the telephone each night checking off their to-do lists for the wedding. Some days were so hectic with work, neither one of them had made any progress. Friday night could not come any too soon for either of them. Moreover, when it did, they decided to wait until Saturday to get together. All Josie could think about is running a hot bubble bath and crawling into bed without setting her alarm.

Grams had insisted Josie invite P.J. to Saturday brunch when she heard they had planned to go ice-skating that afternoon. She said, "I want to make sure you eat a hearty meal before spending the afternoon in the icy cold." Good to her word, she had lavished them with a feast they could not finish. It did seem to give them some extra stream to withstand the icy gusts of wind on the city skating rink. They came home two hours later looking for hot chocolate to help thaw them out.

After church the next morning, Eleanor treated the couple to lunch at the Hurry Back Inn, a little mom-and-pop café in Granite City, just ten minutes south of Lakewood. Then, they headed over to their wedding shower at the Silver Meadows Apartments. The snow was falling, creating a crystalline scene and a snow flurry as they entered the apartment building.

"Good afternoon!" Nellie met them at the security door and escorted them to the community room just down the hall. "How are you today?" A chorus of "Good!" was her answer. "Let me brush the snow off you. The weatherman said to expect snow showers. You may hang your coats along the side there where there are hangers, or you may keep them on a while and drape them over the backs of your chairs when you warm up."

Josie and P.J. thanked her and chose to hang up their coats while Eleanor kept hers on for now.

"You may take your seats at the head table." Nellie gestured toward the one decorated table at the head of the room. "As you can see, a couple of your attendants are already here. Now, if you'll excuse me, I need to tend to something in the kitchen."

The trio went to the head table; passing by a conference table filled with wrapped presents, and greeted the three bridesmaids and the one groomsman who were visiting amongst themselves.

"Hey, Stan!" P.J. greeted his best man with a handshake and sat next to him. Stan was dressed in gray slacks and a black and white ski sweater. Josie was glad he hadn't worn his usual blue jeans and sweatshirt. She glanced down the table to be sure Donna had been just as respectful in her choice of attire, and was just as relieved. No punk-Goth look today; Donna was wearing red corduroy pants and a red and green sweater.

"Hi, girls!" Josie said and sat next to P.J., in the center, yet near her bridesmaids. She hugged Vikki and smiled brightly at Donna and Jessica. "You girls look great! Did you coordinate to wear coordinating colors? You look great in shades of green."

"Hi, Josie!" The girls said and giggled. Donna, always the impertinent one, asked, "So, where's Hildy? Isn't she coming? None of us have spoken to her since Friday."

"No, she's not able to make it today. She had to go home to celebrate Christmas with her parents who were on a cruise most of December," Josie explained.

Just then, a spry silver-haired gentleman in a navy ski sweater and wool pants came up to the table. He was carrying a microphone. He stood on the side of the table between the guests and the gifts and raised the mike to his mouth.

"Greetings one and all! I'm Harvey Citrowske. You may know my daughter-in-law. She's the choir director at St. Andrew's Community Church where our bride has recently sung a couple of solos! I heard them on Christmas Day. She's got a good voice. And, to tell you more about Josie, let's here from her maid of honor, Miss Vikki Dale!" He extended the microphone toward the table while the group of elderly people in the chairs facing them clapped. Vikki stood by her chair and accepted the microphone.

"Hi, I'm Vikki! I work with Josie at Sanderson & Sons, but we've been best friends since primary school! She is the sweetest, most caring person in the world and a great boss. Josie is very creative and is a hard worker. She would never ask any of us to do anything she wouldn't do herself. I'm supposed to tell you a story about when we were kids. Well, Josie found this baby bunny in her back yard once. Her grandmother told her it wouldn't live without its mama, but Josie used her doll bottle to feed it warm milk until it showed an interest in eating grass and lettuce. Then she called the animal control people, who came and took it away to care for it in a way that it could be released back into the wild. I wouldn't call Josie a 'bleeding heart liberal', but she is a true blue friend." Vikki handed the mike back to Harvey and sat down. The audience clapped politely.

"Next, we'll hear from probably the only person, besides Josie, in this town who knows the groom, P.J. Coleson, best. That's his best man, Mr. Stanley Baker." Again, Harvey passed the cordless mike over the table to an attendant. Stan stood and received it with a nod.

"Thanks, Harvey!" Stan said, and cleared his throat. "My buddy, P.J., and I go way back, too. We met in high school. At first, we didn't get along so well. We happened to set our eyes on the same girl. Sorry, Josie," Stan said, looking her way, smiling. "The 'best man' really did win that round, but overall, I'd say P.J. ended up with the best catch. Like, Josie, P.J. is hardworking and as honest as the day is long. He's a knight in shining armor, too, as Josie would attest. Her former boss tried to kill her last year. You may have read about it in the newspaper. Anyway, when Cassandra Coven was holding a gun on Josie, P.J. played Sir Galahad and tackled her, knocking the gun out of her hands. That's the kind of guy my buddy, P.J., is. He's a prince." Stand handed the mike back to Harvey and took a bow when the audience let out a thunderous applause.

"I think most of that is for you," he whispered to P.J., who just shook his head.

Donna jumped up and snatched the microphone from Harvey, leaving him wide-eyed and flustered.

"I want to say something, too," she spoke into the mike. "These two kids are crazy courageous. They not only defeated Cass once, but twice. Josie is so creative she devised a plan for each occasion. First, she made sure Sanderson & Sons got a fitted with security cameras, like all smart businesses, which helped seal the deal in Cass's conviction of murdering old Lew Sanderson. Then, when she knew the FBI wouldn't be able to crack the hard nut Cass was in the . . . accidental death . . . of Eleanor's friend, Josie volunteered to visit the prison, herself, and get Cass to spill her guts. Tell me if that wasn't brave. And, P.J.'s brave for wanting to marry a gal who seems to be a death magnet. It's also a good thing they're good at solving murders." There were some nervous chuckles at that. Looking around the room, Donna seemed to realize what she had just said, and to whom. Her face flushed pink. She added, "And, that's why I'm glad you are honoring them today with this shower." She tossed the microphone back to Harvey, who nearly dropped it, and flopped into her seat. She crossed her arms and leaned back in her chair, working hard not to catch anyone's eye.

Clearing his throat, Harvey said, "Now it's time to play a game. May we have Nellie out here to conduct it, please?" Nellie came up, passing out stacks of scratch paper and pencils on her way to the front. She pulled on the hem of her red and white sweater and accepted the microphone.

"Please put your name at the top of your paper and number from one to ten down the left side," she instructed. "I'll be giving this stainless steel measuring cup set to the person who wins this contest. The winner may do as he or she wishes, but it is customary to regift it to the bridal couple. Are you ready? Here's the first question. What is another word for popular edible fungi? What month comes after March? Next, What is your favorite color? Three: What town are we in? What is the largest city in our state? Name a type of car. What's your favorite number? What is your favorite wild animal? Name another color. What is your age?

"Now, I'm going to read another set of questions, and you will give the answers you have written! Isn't this fun? Here we go! What is P.J.'s favorite room in the house? The mushroom, did you say? Yes! When are they getting married? That's easy, right? April! What color of nightgown will Josie wear on their honeymoon? Probably her favorite color, not yours, right?" Nellie snickered. "Where will the lovebirds live after they get married? Here in Lakewood, of course! Where are they going on their honeymoon? Maybe to Niagara Falls, but likely to New York City. What kind of car will they drive after they've been married and start a family? What did you say? A mini-van? How many children will they have? Did you say, 16?" Nellie looked over at Josie and raised her eyebrows. "What kind of pet will they have? A black panther? A Polar bear! One more. A giraffe! My, you all are so creative! Last question: How long will Josie and P.J. stay married? Did I hear 62? Oh, there's a 78! That's great!" Turning to the bridal couple, Nellie said, "We really do wish you many, many years of wedded bliss!

"Now, who's got all the most right answers?" she asked, turning back to the audience.

One person raised her hand and said, "I have seven!"

"Great! Come up and claim your prize," Nellie said. "Congratulations, Tess! You have won this measuring cup set. Will you keep it, or will you give it to the bridal couple?"

"I'm giving it to Josie and P.J.," Tess said and laid it on the table in front of them.

"Thank you!" P.J. and Josie said together.

Nellie ran another game before having the gifts brought, one by one, to the head table for the bridal party to open, record, and share. When they were done, Harvey got on his trusty microphone again and asked the couple for a speech. They stood together and P.J. took the mike from Harvey.

"I would like to thank everyone of you for the fabulous gifts and the fun games. We are getting married the first Saturday in April and would like you all to come to the dance and kick up your heels to help us celebrate." He passed the mike to Josie, who added, "I want to thank you, too, for all the fun and thoughtfulness of sharing your time with us and for all the very useful gifts. Thanks!"

Then Harvey asked the bridal party to lead the lunch line. So, they enjoyed mock angel food cake with strawberries and whipped topping and coffee and/or blue raspberry punch.

"Did you ever have such fun playing outdated games?" Josie asked P.J. as he took her and Eleanor home after the shower.

"I resent that remark!" Eleanor said, feigning offense. "Nellie asked me for game suggestions. Why, I remember having a blast at my own shower, and showers of my friends, playing those same games."

"I'm sure you did, Grams!" Josie said and giggled.

"We'll just see what kind of shower games the Colesons have you play in New York City next month!"

Chapter Four
Deal With It

On Tuesday, Vikki and Donna, not wanting to be outdone by senior citizens, held a personal shower for Josie over lunch. They had reserved the back room of the café across the street and invited some of Josie's closest women clients. The office workers also arranged to pick up the tab for Josie's lunch, which they later split.

"We decided to hold this impromptu shower on a week day because we wanted to make it R-rated. With P.J.'s twin sisters in school, they wouldn't be able to attend, so they wouldn't be getting 'educated' too soon in life, if you know what I mean," Vikki whispered in Josie's ear as she sat with her at the center of the table. "They said that was fine. They and their mom will be giving you another shower in New York."

"Okay," Josie whispered back, glad the twins weren't here if it was going to be that kind of a shower.

"Nathan sent this card," Donna said, giving it to Josie. "He said his wife would shoot him if he came to a personal shower where the bride was asked to model skimpy lingerie. So, he volunteered to hold down the fort while we're here. He'll take a late lunch when we get back."

"You wouldn't make me model lingerie!" Josie said, wide-eyed with shock.

"No, of course not," Vikki interjected, "but you do have to hold up every gift so we can all see it!"

"Aw, jeez," Josie said, covering her face which was turning as red as the pantsuit she was wearing. "Alright, let's get this over with!"

The girls brought on the presents, each one a little naughtier than the previous one, with the exception of Nathan's. He had simply placed a $20 bill in a very conservative shower card and signed 'Mr. and Mrs. Nathan Danielson and Family'. *How like him to be so proper*, Josie thought.

"Oh, I forgot to give this to you or Vikki earlier!" Donna said, holding up an envelope. "Got the mail for Vikki earlier, so she could come here and get the table set up." She handed it to Josie, who slit it open with the table knife she'd been using as a card opener. There was a single-folded piece of paper in it, instead of a greeting card. She drew it from the envelope and flipped it open. Cutout letters were glued to the inside. They spelled out a warning Josie did not want to share with the others.

DON'T COME TO NEW YORK FOR YOUR SHOWER OR YOU'LL BE SORRY.

Josie gasped slightly, trying not to alarm anyone. Why would anyone send such a threatening note to her at her bridal shower? She stuffed the piece of paper back into the envelope and flipped the envelope over several times to see if she could find a return address or any other markings that would indicate its origin. The only thing she noted was the date stamp read New York, NY. Her fingers trembled as she tried to slide the envelope into her jacket pocket without anyone noticing.

"Who's it from?" Vikki whispered. "Why are you trying to hide it?"

"I'll tell you later," Josie whispered back, smiling at no one in particular. Then, she stood to get everyone's attention. They stopped visiting among themselves. "I want to thank you all for coming to my bridal shower today, and for the—huh hmmm—extremely interesting presents. I'm sure P.J. will have fun watching me model them on our honeymoon. I'm also certain that most of you have to get back to work since you came here on your lunch break. I hope you had fun; I did. Please come help us celebrate our marriage at our wedding dance on the first Saturday night in April. It will be at the Lakewood Community Center. Thanks, again!" As she sat down, she grabbed Vikki by the wrist and said, "Please stay, I have some communication we can catch up on right here."

"Okay! Just let me go pay our bill, and I'll be right back!" Vikki picked up discarded gift-wrap and took it with her to dispose of, her bleach blond locks flowing in the breeze she created. Some of the guests came over and gave Josie a hug on their way out. Each one had a nice compliment to pay her as they wished her well. Vikki returned as the last person walked out the door. Josie took the menacing mail out of her pocket and opened it again. It still said nothing more than it did the first time she read it. She laid the paper in Vikki's outstretched hand.

Vikki read it silently and looked back at Josie, "What in the world . . . ? Who even knows you're going to have shower in New York?"

"I don't know, but I'm not going to disappoint the twins or my future mother-in-law. So, I guess I'll be finding out 'who'." Josie took back the paper and replaced it in the envelope it came in and stuffed it into her purse. Then, she took Vikki's hands in hers and pleaded earnestly. "Vikki, this has got to stay between the two of us. Please don't say a word to anyone. Promise?"

"Yeah, but, you will take that note to the police, won't you? I mean, someone has got to protect you! Plus, as your maid of honor, I'm going with you to New York for that bridal shower, you know. No, don't say 'no'. I'm going, regardless, just like Bess and what's-her-name in those Nancy Drew Mysteries. They didn't back down, and neither will I." They both snickered at that.

"Okay, but do as I say and don't get in the way, okay?" Vikki nodded in agreement. "Okay, then, let's get back to work. Remember, not a word about this to anyone. If we need to discuss it, let's do it in my car, at my place or yours, or at the park. You know, somewhere it's not bugged." The two women picked up their purses and left. As they crossed the street, Vikki stopped Josie and leaned in to whisper in her ear.

"Are you sure you're car isn't bugged?" she asked.

"No, so we'd better not talk there, either," Josie said, "and, we'd better get inside before we catch pneumonia! Remind me not to cross the street in the dead of winter without my coat!" With that the two women rushed across the last half of the street and in through the double-wide glass doors of Sanderson & Sons. For the rest of the week, whenever Josie and Vikki met, they shared a secret smile.

No one thought anything of it since they all knew these two had been best friends forever.

When Josie talked to P.J. on the phone that night, she tried to stay bubbly by talking about the bridal shower and all the naughty little gifts the guests had given her. Yet, there was something nervous about her laughter, and P.J. sensed something was haunting her.

"I can't wait to see you in each and every one of those items," P.J. said, "but, honey, I can tell something's bothering you. Come on, tell ol' P.J. about it."

"Not over the phone," Josie stated flatly. "Why don't you come over Thursday evening, and we'll talk over a cup of hot chocolate?"

"Okay, if I must wait until then, I must. Won't you give me just a little hint? I haven't done anything to upset you, have I? I'll just kick myself if I have."

"No, no. Nothing like that," Josie said. "Just give me a call when you get within two minutes of the house. I'll meet you outside. I don't want Grams to hear. It's a . . . surprise. So, I want to keep it a secret, okay? And, that's why we can't talk about it over the phone; I don't want her to overhear. I'd better go now. Love you."

"Love you, too." P.J. said, and they hung up. Josie left the living room and went into the kitchen on her way up to her room. Eleanor was there with her cornflower blue cobbler's apron on, mixing up bread dough by hand. "Hey, Grams! I don't know why you go through all the trouble of making homemade bread, but I sure do love it that you do!"

"I've made a double batch, so I can make caramel rolls for breakfast, too," Eleanor said. "Would you be a dear and pull out the bread tins and spray them with cooking spray? For some reason I was so excited about the thought of caramel rolls, I only took out the cake pan for them, and not the bread tins."

"No problem," Josie said and demonstrated the fact. "So, how is the painting coming on your apartment? Any idea when it will be ready for you to move in?"

"The building supervisor said he would give me the keys in two weeks. By then the paint will be dry and the new carpet will be laid. As you may recall, I gave them explicit instructions to paint first and lay carpet last."

"Yes, I do remember that," Josie said, smiling. Grams always knew just what order to do things in. "Not to be rushing you or anything, but just how much furniture are you taking? Am I correct in assuming that the apartment isn't that big that I wouldn't have to go buy a lot of new furniture before P.J. moves in, right?"

"That's right, pussycat. It's a one-bedroom apartment, so you can even keep the guest room furniture. I'm thinking about buying a hide-a-bed in case I get overnight company. That way, I won't break up any of the living room or sitting room sets for you, either. You may replace them at your convenience. This kitchen table set is about the only thing I would need from downstairs. You can even keep the large television until P.J. brings over his wide-screen TV. I can get by with the small one from my bedroom."

"That's extremely generous of you, Grams," Josie said, grateful for the diversion from her newest concern regarding the threatening note. "I can put up the card table and chairs until I find a new kitchen set, or will you be taking that with you too? P.J. and I can go shopping for a set right away."

"You'll probably get a card table and chairs for a wedding present, so don't go out and buy one of those. If you meant a kitchen set, that's a different story. That would be a good investment." Eleanor turned three new loaves of bread into the tins Josie had prepared. Josie took them and placed them into the preheated oven. Then, Eleanor returned to the messy cupboard and started rolling out more dough and spreading brown sugar, cinnamon and pats of butter on it. After which, she rolled it into a log shape and cut off one-inch thick pinwheels and laid them flat in the cake pan. Josie had picked up the plastic wrap box and marked out a sheet that would cover the cake pan. Eleanor always put the unbaked rolls into the refrigerator until morning, at which time she would bake them fresh for breakfast.

"Thank you, dear," Eleanor said as she closed the refrigerator door. "It's nice to be baking with you in the kitchen again. It's been a while."

"I know. I'm usually in the dining room pouring over work I brought home." Josie wiped her hands on a towel and held it for Eleanor while she washed her hands in the kitchen sink. "I even brought some home tonight, but after P.J. called, I just couldn't focus anymore."

"Ah, young love," Eleanor said with a sigh. Josie seized the given excuse and agreed. They smiled at each other, and Josie gave her grandmother a hug.

"Well, I'm off to bed, Grams. It's been an exciting day, what with the shower, and all. I'll be looking forward to those caramel rolls for breakfast."

"Goodnight, dear. Sweet dreams." Eleanor turned back to the counter to start cleaning, and Josie dragged herself up the back steps to her bedroom.

As she undressed for bed, Josie realized she wasn't tired yet, so she took a shower and laid out her clothes for the next day. She selected the navy skirt suit Sherri Ingram had made for her when she returned to Lakewood earlier that year to take back her late father's company. The reception Sid Silverstein, the estate lawyer, threw, had attracted a large crowd of townspeople since no one knew the identity of Lew Sanderson's heir. Sherri had done a superb job on the scrollwork on the jacket and even gave Josie a discount coupon for an elite shoe store in New York City where she found a matching pair of pumps. Josie's face brightened some when she remembered how it felt to have Sid introduce her to everyone as Lew's sole heir, Cass's thunderous face, and how the mayor welcomed her with the key to the city. She also shivered when she remembered how frightened she was as she realized how close she came to being killed by Cass over the whole deal.

That thought brought her full-circle to the current threat. She lay in bed wondering, Just what was she going to do? Thursday couldn't come quick enough, as far as Josie was concerned. She hated keeping secrets from P.J. At least he knows she was keeping one.

Wednesday drug on and on relentlessly. She called Vikki into to her office ten times more than usual just to share that secret smile, but then shake her head and make up something for Vikki to do. Josie was tempted to skip choir rehearsal that night, but too many people would wonder why. She could say she was sick again, but that would be lying. Josie couldn't bring herself to do that, either. She remembered playing hooky from school once. It was horrible keeping that secret. It wasn't like she had had anything special to do, or caused any other trouble for herself. In fact, she had just taken a sketchbook to the park and did some fall color sketches for the last period of the day, which was study hall. So, it wasn't like she'd missed out on a class lecture. However, she felt so guilty, she confessed to her grandmother that very night. So, there was no question about it, Josie was going to choir rehearsal whether she felt like it or not.

That night, lying awake in her bed again, Josie reviewed in her mind all the near-scrapes she had had this year. It had been quite a year of murder, mystery and mayhem. If Andy Hoverstein hadn't fitted the office with recording cameras, and P.J. hadn't arrived when he had that fateful night, she'd be dead right now.

Andy! Why hadn't she thought of him before? Josie sprang from the bed and flew to her dresser. She dug through her jewelry box until she found Andy's business card. He told her to call him if she ever found herself in another pickle like she had been with Cass. He would be only too willing to help her solve the dilemma, if the FBI didn't have him on assignment out of state. Glancing at the clock, which read 9:45 p.m., Josie snatched up her cellphone and dialed Andy's number.

"I'm on another call or way from my desk at the moment," Andy's tenor voice came on the line. "Please leave your name, number and a brief message after the beep, and I will get back to you as soon as possible." *Beep.*

"Hi, Andy! It's Josie Buchannon. I don't know if you remember me or not, but you said I could call if ever I was 'in a pickle' like last winter with Cass. Please call me; I need your advice. My cell number is 212-555-0515." Hopefully, he would be able to return her call before she talked to P.J. Thursday night. She saved Andy's number in her cellphone database and crawled back into bed. There was nothing left to do now, but to deal with it until they could get a plan together.

Chapter Five
"Planning is what I do best!"

Andy didn't call Josie back until she was on the way home from work Thursday afternoon. *Nothing like taking his sweet time to return my call,* Josie thought as she answered the phone, then realized that an FBI operative like Andy couldn't just pick up a phone and call an old case victim any time he well pleased.

"Hey, Josie! This is Andy Hoverstein," he said. "I got your message. I'm sorry I didn't return your call until now. I was on assignment until a half hour ago. Just got out of debriefing. What's up?"

"Andy, I'm so glad you called. The other day I got a mysterious note in the mail, warning me to stay out of New York City. Andy, I've got a bridal shower there in a couple of weeks. Whoever sent the note must have known about it.

I'm scared. I'm meeting with my fiancé tonight and telling him about it. My maid of honor knows too. She wants me to take the note to the police."

"You haven't done that, yet?" Andy asked. "That probably should have been your first step. Has anyone handled the note but you?"

"One of my employees brought it to me from the post office. Then, when I showed it to Vikki, my maid of honor, she held it, too, but that's it."

"Okay. Just don't let anyone else touch it. Take it straight to the police station and give it to someone you trust. And, outside of your fiancée, don't tell another person about it. Tell him and your maid of honor not to tell anyone, either. Swear them to secrecy at all costs. Now, what's the date of your shower and where?" She told him. "Okay, I've got it. Do whatever your police department says. Give them my name and number and have them contact me with their plans. Above all, don't worry. I'll make sure I'm around that weekend, so I can keep an eye on you. Relax, you hear? The more nervous or worried you are, the more people will notice."

"Okay, I'll do as you say. Thanks! I really appreciate it!" Josie said.

"If you need to reach me, try to do it when no one who doesn't know about this is around. It may even be best to make the call when you're outside, like in a park or something. Let me know if you get any more correspondence."

"Will do. Thanks, again!" Josie said. They said goodbye and hung up. Josie pulled a U-turn and headed to the police station. Along the way, she call them and asked for Sgt. Rachel Rodriguez, who was helpful last fall when Eleanor's friend, Virginia Fieney, had been murdered in the Buchannons' sitting room.

"She's out for supper right now, but she should be back in about 15 minutes," the receptionist told Josie. "Can I have her call you back?"

"No, that's okay," Josie replied. "I'm coming down to the station now. I'll just wait for her." When she got off the phone with the receptionist, Josie dialed P.J.'s number. She was just going to tell him where she was going, but then thought better of it. Why not have him meet her at the station? P.J. answered, and Josie said, "P.J., honey, I got hold of Andy Hoverstein, do you remember him from Cass's arrest? Anyway, he told me to go to the police department to see Sgt. Rachel about something. Why don't you meet me there?"

"Good thing you caught me," P.J. said. "I was about to pull into the parking lot at my apartment. I'll be right there. Does this have anything to do with what you were going to tell me about tonight?"

"Yes, but please don't ask anything else. I don't know if our phones or vehicles have been bugged. Please help me remember to ask Sgt. Rachel if they can check for that. See you there. 'Bye." Josie hung up before P.J. could ask her any more questions. He had plenty when they met in the parking lot of the Lakewood Police Station.

"Alright, Josie, this has gone on long enough," P.J. said after their quick peck of a greeting. "I'm starting to get worried. Why all the secrecy? What's going on? Why couldn't we talk on our cellphones? Had your cellphone been missing?"

"No, but someone knows I'm going to New York for your mom's bridal shower, and they don't like it. I got this note through the mail the other day. It said, "Don't go to New York for your bridal shower. If you do, you'll be sorry.' Last night I remembered I had Andy Hoverstein's phone number and called it. I'm sorry I couldn't tell you before this. Andy convinced me to bring the note to the police. I called ahead to talk with Sgt. Rachel. You remember her, she handled Virginia's case."

"Yes, I do remember her. She was so good with your grandmother right after the accident. Okay, let's go in. I can hear the rest along with Sgt. Rachel." P.J. opened the front door of the police station and let Josie go in ahead of him. "Besides, your lips are starting to turn blue from the cold."

"I think it's just the fluorescent lighting," Josie said, entering ahead of him. "But I won't complain about getting inside. I'm beginning to hate winter."

Soon, Sgt. Rachel had shown Josie and P.J. into the same conference room they had met with the FBI agents regularly during the investigation into Virginia's murder. They removed their winter coats and hung them on a coat rack near the conference room door.

"Would you like some coffee?" Sgt. Rachel asked and started pouring when they nodded. Setting the cups on the table in front of them, she took a seat across the table. "Now, how can I help you?"

Josie drew the note from her purse and passed it across to the police officer. Sgt. Rachel pulled a pair of rubber gloves from her pocket and put them on before she opened the envelope and read the message.

"It came in the mail on Tuesday," Josie said. "As you can see, there's no return address or signature, or anything that would indicate who sent it."

"How many people know you're going to New York?"

"I don't know for sure. It depends on if Mrs. Coleson has sent out her invitations yet, or not."

"I can help with that," P.J. said. "I called home last night, and Mom said she had had them mailed yesterday.

She said a co-worker had helped her address them, and she volunteered to mail them. So Mom let her."

"How many people have handled this?" Sgt. Rachel held up the freaky note.

"My employee, Donna Schmidt, had gotten the mail. She handled it, and so did my best friend, Vikki, with whom I shared it after the shower here, at the café, Tuesday. When I called Andy last night, that's FBI Agent Andy Hoverstein, he told me not to let anyone else touch it, so P.J. hasn't seen it either. Would you please show him?" Sgt. Rachel turned the note around and opened it. She held it until P.J. had finished reading it, then she put it back into the envelope and set it on the table. She picked up the headset on the nearby telephone and punched a couple of numbers.

"Please come in and run some evidence to the lab for me. And bring in two notebooks with pens, please." She hung up the receiver and returned her attention to Josie and P.J. "We'll test it for fingerprints, but because you, Donna, Vikki, and several postal workers touched it, it may be a dead end."

"Not to mention the suspect may have worn gloves," P.J. added. They all nodded to that.

"Can you think of any one you met in New York, someone you may have worked with or met at the YMCA or at church that may have had a grudge against you? Anyone who saw you as a threat with the way you moved up so quickly?"

"I met so few people in that company, I wouldn't know of anyone there. I wasn't there long enough to really be a threat to anyone." Josie's eyes rolled back as she thought. "The only one I was a threat to, that I know of, was Cass. And she's in solitary confinement."

"How about you, P.J.? You're from New York. Any idea who might feel threatened by Josie going back there?" Sgt.

Rodriguez asked. She leaned forward over her notebook to gaze at him.

"Nope. Everyone I know loves Josie," P.J. said shaking his head. "She's never done anyone wrong as long as I've known her. She's not a practical jokester, nor does she make fun of people—even behind their backs. I know that makes her sound like a saint, and she's probably not. But then, I'm probably a little biased."

"True that," Josie interjected, smiling.

"Well, we'll run the note for fingerprints or anything else they might find. I will call you and Agent Hoverstein when the results are back. You said he would watch over you in New York? That's good because that's out of our jurisdiction. If you think of anything else in the meantime, please call me." With that, Sgt. Rodriguez walked them to the door.

On the way home, Josie and P.J. talked with each other on their cellphones about her impending trip to New York. It would come up fast enough, and they had to have a plan in place.

"Come on, sweetie! You came up with two great plans when it came to luring Cass out," P.J. said. "I know you'll think of something for the bridal shower in New York, too."

"Yeah, probably. After all, that's what I do best: Plan ahead."

Josie had trouble sleeping that night. Her head was swimming with visions of various ways her New York bridal shower could end in her demise: Poisoned punch, exploding cake, masked gunmen bursting into the conference room. The only way she was going to feel safe was if her two heroes were there, too. If only P.J. and Andy were bridesmaids . . .

Josie went into work early the next morning hoping to get some work done. For a while, it worked because there was no one else there. The peace and quiet added to the familiarity of her office. However, when the others started filtering in and the phones started ringing, Josie started feeling agitated. It was the last straw when Vikki brought in the mail.

"I've opened and date-stamped everything, Josie, so you don't have to concern yourself with that," Vikki whispered as she handed a stack to Josie. "There's nothing bad in there."

Josie glanced up into Vikki's face as she reached for the mail. She could see the worry in her friend's eyes.

"Thank you, Vikki," Josie said, starting to pick through the envelopes. "I really appreciate the trouble you're going through for me."

"You want to do lunch with me today?" Vikki asked, trying to act like her bubbly self. "We could do a picnic in the park . . ."

"Okay, but I'll have to pick up a to-go package from the café. Let me order that right now," Josie said, setting down the mail. "You go on and get back to work. I'll be fine." Josie dialed the number for the restaurant across the street as she watched Vikki disappear through the door. She ordered a turkey and ham sandwich and a Special K bar to go at noon and hung up.

Going back to the mail, Josie was on autopilot as she sorted it, her mind on the mysterious message from the other day. *Some people really know how to take the fun out of reading the mail*, she thought. Looking down, she realized she hadn't sorted anything at all as she ended up with just one pile. Setting the mail aside, she pulled her steno pad and pen to her and started doodling.

Vikki, Donna and Jessica were coming with to New York. Hildy begged off again because she had a date. That didn't come around very often, she admitted to Josie, and she didn't want to pass up the opportunity. She gave Josie two shower gifts to make up for missing the showers. Josie excused her.

In her notebook, Josie wrote: Short one attendant at shower. Hefty attendant, who didn't always wear makeup, seldom wore a dress. Cross that out, Never wears a dress. Hmmm.

By noon, a new plan had begun to form. Josie had filled three pages in her notebook with the idea that had started to gel.

In the park later, Josie and Vikki were glad they had ordered sandwiches because it was hard to eat with their gloves on. Thanks to the mid-winter thaw, though, the temperature was mild enough to have their picnic.

Josie hadn't gotten through the first half of her sandwich before Vikki started interrogating her.

"What did the police say about your note? Have you heard back on their test results? What are they going to do about it? Can they send a body guard with us to the bridal shower in New York City?"

"Whoa, slow down and let me catch up!" Josie exclaimed. "No, Sgt. Rodriguez hasn't called me with the results yet. No, they can't send a bodyguard with us because the Big Apple is out of their jurisdiction. But, do you remember FBI Agent Andy Hoverstein? I called him Wednesday night, and he said he would keep an eye on me in New York City."

"Ooh! That blond hotty who wired the office? I can't wait to see him again!" Vikki gushed.

"Yeah, well, maybe you will and maybe you won't. It will depend on how visible he will be," Josie said. "I've got an idea he may be working undercover on this one as well."

Chapter Six
Spiced Apple

"This is Josie Buchannon," Josie answered her cell phone that evening. "How can I help you?"

"This is Agent Hoverstein," Andy answered. "I'm on my way to Lakewood and would like to meet you somewhere in a neighboring town. There's a town north of you and one south of you. Which one do you frequent enough no one would think twice about you being there, but may not know you're engaged, or if they do, what he looks like?"

"Right! There's this great mom-and-pop café on Main Street Deer Valley to the north. Did you want me to come tonight or over lunch tomorrow, when I usually go there?"

"Lunch tomorrow sounds good. I'll see you then!"

Josie was starting to get goose bumps. She could barely wait until lunch the next day when she and Andy could get a plan together to protect her from this crazy note writer.

At precisely 11:45 a.m. Josie whizzed by the front desk and called to Vikki over her shoulder, "I'm going to lunch out of town. Not sure when I'll get back. I'll call you if I'm going to be out the rest of the day."

"Don't go dress shopping without me!" Vikki called after her.

"No worries," Josie replied and slipped out the door. She would have run to her car and roared out of town, but she neither wanted to slip on the ice nor get a speeding ticket. So, she just bided her time. Whew! Josie breathed a sigh of relief when she reached city limits and a freeway speed limit. She concentrated on setting the cruise control. She didn't want to be late for her appointment with an FBI agent.

Andy was already in a booth toward the back of the café when Josie arrived. She sat across from him and picked up the menu that lay on the table.

"Hi, Josie. How've you been?" Andy greeted her. He took a sip of his coffee. Josie noticed he was wearing a chambray work shirt and blue jeans and wondered if he always dressed so casually.

"I'm fine, all things considered," she answered. "I'm getting a little concerned about this new threat, though. What kind of horrible things could this person dream up that would make me sorry for going to my own bridal shower?" She pulled off her gloves, eased out of her wool coat and picked up the menu again. Just then the waitress came over with the coffee pot and a cup. She set them on the table and smiled.

"Would you like coffee or maybe some hot chocolate? Aren't you the lady who likes whipped cream on her hot chocolate?"

"Yes, I am, and that sounds wonderful. Please." Josie smiled back at the server who nodded and left to get Josie's beverage of choice.

"Have you ordered?" Josie asked Andy. "What are you having?"

"No, I waited to order my meal until you came. You eat here, right? What do you recommend?"

"Today's special. I like to come here a lot during the week for their specials. The cook does an excellent job on these everyday meals, like the homemade meatloaf today. That's what I'll have." She told the waitress the same thing when her hot chocolate arrived.

"I'll have the same, and put hers on my tab," Andy said. The waitress winked at him and left. "So, we have to go to New York City together. I'll be your bodyguard the entire weekend. The only thing that bugs me is that I'll be out of place at the shower unless it's for guys too."

"No, it's not. And that's why I came up with the Spiced Apple Plan," Josie said.

"Just hold on a minute. 'Spiced Apple'? That sounds a little risqué," Andy said, leaning in to whisper.

"Only the name is spicy," Josie said. "I thought of calling it 'Blond Hotty' because of something my receptionist said, but thought that was a little too much."

"You're darned tootin' it's too much," Andy shook his head, his blond bangs tossed to and fro. Josie brushed her own chestnut bangs from her eyes and then reached for her notebook from beside her on the bench seat. She had dropped it there along with her purse when she first sat down. She opened it and slid it across the table toward Andy.

He must have seen the waitress coming with their meal as he flipped the notebook upside down to prevent her from seeing its contents.

"Two meatloaf dinners," Flo said as she set them down in front of Josie and Andy. "Any dessert right now, or should I check back with you later?"

"Later," Andy and Josie said at the same time. They smiled at each other, then at Flo. She nodded and left to wait on someone who had just arrived.

Andy picked up the notebook and turned it back over. There was just one page with the title, Spiced Apple. He took a few moments to read it before speaking. When he finished, he looked up into Josie's crystal blue eyes and snickered.

"You can't be serious," he said.

"I am," she replied. "And what's so funny? Haven't you ever gone undercover like that?"

"In drag? Once or twice to bring down prostitution rings, but nothing else. Let's see if I remember which one of your employees Hildy is. Hmm. She'd have to be one of the two tallest chicks in your place. And since I'm not the skinniest guy around, that leaves only the production lady. You know, with the right wig, I could probably pull it off. Just don't expect me to wear a dress."

"That's what Hildy said when I asked her to be in my wedding!" They laughed. "Actually, not wearing a dress, you wouldn't have to shave your legs, either, and since she doesn't wear much make-up, you won't have to get too painted up. I take that back, with that five o'clock shadow, you might have to really pack it on!" They laughed again.

"I'll take this plan back to my supervisor and get his opinion. Then I'll give you a call to set it in motion." With that, he dug into his meatloaf and they enjoyed the rest of their dinner without any more shop talk.

The waitress stopped by to top off Andy's coffee and ask if they wanted dessert. Instead, Andy dug into his jeans pocket and pulled out cash for both their lunches. He even gave Flo a hefty tip and sent her away humming. Then Andy and Josie slipped their coats back on and left.

When Josie returned to the office, she stopped by Vikki's desk for her messages. There were only two. One from the city maintenance manager informing her they would be flushing the sewer main for the main street district on Saturday and requesting no one from the business come into the office to work over the weekend. The other didn't have a return address. The postmark was from New York City. Chills ran up Josie's spine. She shivered.

"What's wrong," Vikki asked. She must not have looked through the mail closely, Josie thought. Without much more thought she winked soberly and tilted her head in the direction of her office. She walked into the production room without looking back. She didn't have to. The wink had become the BFFs' secret code for "DANGER". Vikki would be on her heals as soon as she could grab a notebook to make it look legit.

Inside her own office, Josie shed her coat and put her purse in her desk drawer. She sat in her office chair and opened the mysterious envelope. Vikki shut the door behind her and pulled up a folding chair. She sat and leaned over the desk with a question mark on her face.

"Just as I suspected," Josie said, not looking up. Whispering, she read the contents of the note that was pieced together like the first. "**IF YOU DON'T STAY AWAY, SOMEONE WILL GO MISSING.**" Vikki's tiny hands flew to her cheeks, and she gasped.

"Who do you think will go missing? Who's sending you these notes? What are you going to do about it?" Vikki asked.

"What can I do about it? We can't catch the person if we don't go ahead with our plan." Josie replied. "Who's to say they won't kidnap someone anyway? If not one of my friends or relatives, then he could get someone else. This person has to be stopped before he hurts someone!"

"Or she," Vikki added. She flipped her bleached blond hair behind her shoulder and asked, "You mentioned a plan. Whose plan? What's it about?"

Josie craned her neck around Vikki to see if anyone was watching them through the open window. No one was. Then she looked down at the base of the door. There was a slight break between the bottom of the door and the floor under it. Light often shone through that crack under the door, when no one blocked it by standing in front of the door. The light was shining well enough, so she leaned over the desk, too, and whispered, "Agent Andy Hoverstein will be dressing as Hildy for the shower. Don't you tell a soul or our friendship is over."

"Oh, I won't tell a soul!" Vikki swore.

"You had better not. If this leaks out, you won't be my maid of honor."

"That's cold," Vikki said, pouting.

"Reality can be cold. Our lives depend on this. You are the only other person, besides P.J., that will know. Oh! I haven't told him, yet, either. I hope he forgives me for telling you before I told him! Now, scoot! Back to work with you! I have to call P.J."

Vikki made the motion for zipping her lip and took her leave. Josie pulled out her cell phone and texted P.J. that they had to meet at the park after work. She had already warned him it may come to that, so she didn't think he would be surprised to see the message. She wasn't surprised, either, when a short time later, she received a single-letter text response: 'K'.

The afternoon moved at a snail's pace as Josie was torn between working on her ad sketches and thinking about her new plan, The Spiced Apple. Once she even shook her head at the absurdity of the plan name. She hoped it didn't sound as stupid to Andy. He didn't say anything or act like he didn't like it. Maybe the FBI gave plans their own names, so they can claim credit for them. She had her doubts, though. She couldn't believe they would spend time, energy and money sitting around renaming other people's plans.

Josie managed to deliver two presentations that afternoon and got approval to move ahead with the projects. For the rest of the afternoon, she was able to surf the web and pretend she was doing research for a new campaign. Finally it was four forty-five, and Josie flew out of the office faster than she had for lunch. She couldn't wait to share the new information with P.J.

As she stepped into her car to warm it up before going home, Josie's cellphone rang. "This is Josie. How can I help you?" she said, thinking it was one of her few clients she'd given her cellphone number to because they always called at the last second, but they were high-value accounts.

"This is Sid, Josie. How are you today?" the lawyer asked.

"Oh, it's you," she said dully.

"And, a good evening, to you too!" he answered, non-plused. "From your tone, I take it you haven't spoken to P.J., yet about the prenuptial agreement."

Chapter Seven
Getting Down to Business

"No, I'm sorry. I haven't," Josie said with a sigh, wishing Sid hadn't called to remind her about the prenuptial agreement he insisted P.J. sign before too long. "It's been pretty busy around here. We've got another situation around here. Or, rather in New York. Please contact Agent Hoverstein for details."

"Sorry to hear about that," Sid's voice changed it's tone to sympathetic. "I will messenger over a copy of the pre-nup, with all the signature places marked for both you and P.J. Just sign them in front of a notary public and mail them back, or bring them into the office. If I'm not here, my assistant can notarize them for you. I will then get them registered at the courthouse. Please don't dilly-dally. We want to make sure the papers are filed before you get married."

"Understood." The conversation turned briefly to the weather and the number of new clients Josie had signed for Sanders & Sons since the first of the year.

"How's your grandmother doing?" Sid asked.

"Grams is doing remarkably well," Josie replied. "She will be moving into a senior high rise next week. She's really looking forward to living just down the hall from her friends. With winter upon us, it will make it that much easier for her to get to her Bridge Club game days and other entertainment."

'Oh, really? Please tell her if they're ever short a player, she could call me." With Josie's promise to relay the message, Sid said goodbye.

In the short time it took Josie to return to her office, a messenger was standing in front of her waiting for her signature on the receipt form before handing over the document her lawyer had promised. Josie reluctantly signed and exchanged the clipboard for the dreaded package.

"Thanks," she mumbled and fished a dollar tip out of her desk drawer.

"Thank you," the young woman in a necktie and menswear suit said, "but, I'm not allowed to take tips. Lawyers frown upon that as 'unprofessional'. Oh, don't worry; Mr. Silverstein pays me well enough. Good day!" With that, she left the office at the next thing to a sprint.

"I can see you must be worth it, being so fast that I'm now talking to thin air," Josie mused, then opened the envelope in front of her. The four-page document that slid out wasn't quite as formidable as she thought it was. Glancing through it, she was impressed anew at the immensity of her holdings. Lew had amassed quite a nest egg that included most of main street, a mansion of a house that Josie had planned to sell as soon as she could find a buyer and of course, Sanderson & Sons Advertising Agency. Josie drew a deep, cleansing breath and let it out slowly. She really could understand why Sid was so concerned. Well, she might as well get this over with, she thought and dialed P.J.'s cellphone number.

"Hello, Josie," P.J. whispered in her ear. He was breathing heavily, like he was working hard to get to a private location. Josie recalled his favorite place to take private calls was in the men's room, which in turn reminded her of the time Ray had changed the restroom signs on P.J. and he walked into the ladies room by mistake. She chuckled under her breath.

"Hi, sweetie! Can you come over tonight instead of meeting at the park? Sid sent some papers over for us to sign."

"I was just about to call you to say we may have to meet after 8 o'clock. Suddenly I have a supper meeting at five-thirty."

"That's fine. We'll save you some dessert." Josie smiled.

That was settled. She stuffed the envelope with the pre-nup into her briefcase to take home with her and reached for her coat one more time.

< * >

At home, she helped Grams with supper by setting the table and pouring milk.

"Is something troubling you, pussycat?" Grams asked tentatively, wiping her hands on her paisley print apron. "You've barely said two words since you got home."

"Oh, Grams! Sid called today and reminded me I have to ask P.J. to sign a pre-nuptial agreement; then he sent it right over by messenger. I hope you don't mind that I've asked P.J. to come for dessert later. I've got to tell him."

"No problem, dear. You know there's always enough for him to come over. You could have asked him to supper, too."

"I would have, but he has a dinner meeting going on until close to eight o'clock. He'll stop by when it's over."

"So, he's getting high up into management that he's taking in 'dinner meetings', now, eh?"

"It's not quite like that," Josie shook her head. "He's going along just to observe. Anyway, if Lew hadn't left me quite so much, I wouldn't even consider it. Having him sign such a document just kind of smacks the face of love."

"I know, dear," Grams said, patting Josie's forearm, "however, Sid is the expert on these things. You have to trust his counsel. How is he these days, anyway?"

"He sounded fine. In fact, he said if you ever need another card player to give him a call." Josie gave her grandmother a quick hug before going to the refrigerator for butter and jam. Grams had baked hot-crossed buns to go with the homemade stew for supper.

"That was sweet of him. I may have to take him up on that," Eleanor said as she picked up the soup ladle and filled two bowels before sitting at the table. Josie joined her. They said their table prayer and began to eat.

Josie helped her grandmother with the dishes and they retired to the living room to watch a couple of half hour comedy on television while Josie waited for P.J.'s arrival.

"Grams, there's also a—situation—I need to talk to P.J. about privately when he arrives," Josie said during a commercial. "Do you suppose you could take your time when you go to the kitchen to dish up dessert?"

"Certainly, dear," Eleanor agreed, her voice filled with concern. Turning toward Josie, she asked, "Do I need to worry? You aren't getting cold feet, are you, Josie?"

"Oh, no, Grams! I'm delighted to be marrying P.J. It's getting harder and harder to be apart from him! No, it's more of an FBI nature. Something's up that I can't talk about. Just know that Andy's on the job, okay?"

"That does make me feel better," Eleanor said and nodded.

"Just don't tell anyone anything, will you? You know how sensitive things like this are."

"Oh, don't worry about me. What do I know, anyway? You haven't told me anything!" She smiled at her granddaughter. She knew better than to pry or to try to be overprotective. Josie had already survived two murder investigations and an attempt on her life. And, Andy Hoverstein knew his job. Josie would be as safe as she could ever be under similar circumstances, Eleanor had to believe.

Just then the doorbell chimed and P.J. walked into the house. He pulled off his coat and wiped his snow-covered feet before joining the ladies in the family room. He threw his coat over a straight back chair and gave Eleanor a hug in greeting.

"Two of my favorite women!" he said, and walked over to the couch to give his bride-to-be a smooch. "How are you ladies tonight?"

"Good!" they chimed, beaming at him.

"How was your meeting?" Eleanor asked. "Josie mentioned you were able to observe a dinner meeting tonight. It sounds like you're making points with your supervisor."

"Aw, I don't know about that, but the meeting went well. I took some notes and enjoyed a stuffed pork chop dinner. It probably wasn't as good as whatever you two had, but it was good."

"Would you still have room for homemade apple pie and ice cream?" Eleanor tempted him.

"Oh, I think I can make room for a piece of that!" P.J. winked at his soon-to-be grandmother-in-law and helped her out of her recliner.

"I'll go see if it's cooled off enough to cut," Eleanor said.

"Thank you. I would appreciate that very much." He and Josie watched as Eleanor left the room then looked back at each other. P.J. sat next to Josie on the couch and looked into her eyes, his brows furrowed. "What kind of documents did Sid send over? It's too early to sign our marriage certificate."

"Yes, that is true," Josie answered. Reaching for her briefcase, she drew out the manila envelope bearing the lawyer's return address. She pulled the document out and handed it to P.J. before saying any more. "Sid is insistent that I get you to sign this pre-nuptial agreement. P.J., look me in the eye, please. I want you to see my face as I tell you that this was not my idea. I wouldn't dream of asking you to do this if Sid hadn't advised it. I also want to apologize for not telling you about it sooner. He actually brought it up right before New Year's Eve, but I didn't want to spoil the holiday for us with this—business."

Josie's expression pleaded silently with P.J. to be understanding and forgiving. Her heart pounded in fear that he would disapprove, maybe even get upset and storm out. She was only presenting it on her lawyer's insistence. If the estate weren't so large, and Sid such a good lawyer, she wouldn't have bothered.

"Oh, honey! No worries!" P.J. took her in his arms and held her tightly for a moment. "Hey, my dad had to ask my mom to sign one, too, when they got married. It's okay. I'll sign it. Here, let me get my pen out, and we'll do it right now." He reached inside his sport coat and drew out a sparkly silver pen. He skimmed through the document to the first signing spot.

"Sorry, P.J.," Josie stopped him by putting her hand on his. "We have to do it in front of a notary public, either at the city office or at Sid's office."

"Oh, yeah! I forgot that. No problem, let's do lunch tomorrow and take care of it then, okay?" She nodded and he leaned over and kissed her. After a second, she pushed him away.

"That's not all," Josie said, shaking her head, her chestnut mane swaying from side to side. "I met with Andy at noon today, and we went over my idea for him to come to the shower in New York. When we go to lunch tomorrow, I will tell you all about it."

"Ooh, yeah." P.J. suddenly got serious. He squeezed her shoulder with the arm that had been draped over the back of the overstuffed couch. "That's right; we were going to be extra careful about spilling secrets in that regard, weren't we? Okay, so we'll be getting take-out and eating on the road so we can spend a little extra time at Sid's office. I'm sure that's a secure place to talk."

At that point, Eleanor walked into the room carrying the dessert tray, teacups steaming and ice cream beginning to melt on the still-warm pie.

"Are you all talked out and ready to sweeten things up with this bedtime snack?" Eleanor asked. P.J. jumped up to take the heavy tray from her and set it on the coffee table.

"This sure is just what the doctor ordered!" P.J. said, just a little too brightly. He handed the women their plates before picking up his. They all sat back and enjoyed the treat and watched a rerun of Three's Company, one of Eleanor's favorite TV shows.

True to his word, P.J. picked up Josie at work just after 12 noon and took her through a fast food place and to the park where they could discuss more wedding plans, in addition to signing the prenuptial agreement. Josie didn't know why she ever worried about P.J.'s reaction to signing the pre-nup. She had even mentioned it to her grandmother hat she thought Mr. and Mrs. Paul Coleson had probably signed one. She was relieved that he had confirmed the assumption. She was able to eat her lunch without any further concern.

Sid's assistant, Amy, offered them coffee, which they accepted. Josie thought it may give them the reason they needed for sticking around longer than it took to sign the documents before them. Amy summarized the contents of the document and pointed to the signature lines on four copies.

"There's one copy for each of you, one for the courthouse and one for our files," she explained and handed each of them a pen so that they could be signing at the same time. They accepted the writing instruments and made short work of the signatures while Amy worked her stamp. It reminded Josie of an assembly line.

"Do you mind if we stay in here and finish our coffee before we leave?" Jose asked Amy when they were finished signing their names.

"No problem," the assistant said. "I will shut the door on my way out, so you have some privacy."

The second the door clicked behind Amy, Josie turned to P.J. and filled him in on the Spiced Apple undercover project Andy was going to undertake.

"Hoverstein, in a wig and makeup! I can't wait to see that!" P.J. exclaimed. "At least he has a stocky woman to portray and doesn't have to wear a dress!"

"Now you know," Josie said, giving her fiancé a wink and smiled.

"Now I know! And, now, it's time I got back to work!" They drained their coffee cups and left.

Chapter Eight
New Year's Resolutions

January was nearly over, but Josie sat at her desk with her head buzzing over the travel plans she had to make for the upcoming trip to New York for her bridal shower. She had just gotten off the phone with a hotel clerk who had told her they were all booked up for the weekend the Colesons were holding the bridal shower. There was going to be some cutlery convention in the area and hotels within a 60-mile radius were totally booked. Would she like to be placed on a waiting list? Josie finally said yes to the last clerk she spoke with, but had her doubts they would get down to her name. She hung up disappointed.

Josie leaned back and took out her trusty steno pad. She reached into her purse for her special thinking pen. It was a bright royal blue with stretches of brightly colored paisley, like those fancy Russian Easter Eggs.

I have to clear my head somehow, Josie thought. *I'm not going to get any work done worrying about this trip. It will unfold as it will.* Only God knew how it would turn out, but it had to be done. *I should've made a New Year's Resolution not to get involved in anymore investigations.* Nodding, she put pen to paper, writing,

New Year's Resolutions:

1. Be it resolved, I will take on no more investigations after this shower thing.
2. Be it resolved, I will lose five pounds before the wedding.
3. Be it resolved I will make time to shop for my wedding dress while in New York . . . if I get time.
4. Be it resolved I will learn how to cook like Grams.
5. Be it resolved I will spend more time on wedding plans and get things done!

Just how many resolutions were people supposed to make? Josie wondered. *That had better be it for now,* she told herself. *I have work to do!* She pulled her sketch pad toward her and bent over it to finish the commercial she had been working on. There had been way too many distractions lately. She had clients clamoring for their ads, and with the new clients they had added this month, Josie would be taking work home with her for a while. She reached over and made a note on her steno pad to call Mrs. Coleson and ask for room to put up her bridesmaids when they arrived for the shower. With Andy coming undercover, Josie had hoped to get a hotel room, but that was not going to happen. She would just have to find a discreet way to tell Mrs. Coleson Andy as Hildy needed "her" own room—maybe the loft above the garage! No, that's where P.J. would be staying. Well, maybe the den. No, that's where the twins would be sleeping. Mrs. Coleson had already assigned those places, with Josie and Vikki in P.J.'s room and the other bridesmaids in the twin's room, with a cot. Maybe Andy could just sleep on the couch in the living room or switch with the twins. They can sleep in the living room and Andy in the den. That's it. That's where he will have to sleep. Josie made a note of that, too, on her steno pad, and was able to go back to concentrating on her job.

"Josie, you've been working too hard," Vikki said as she bounced into Josie's office with the mail. Josie looked up with a smile. Vikki flipped back her bleach blond hair, which she must have used a a curling iron on that morning, or it would have gone straight again. "We should do lunch today and plan what we're wearing for that bridal shower in New York. I know you're the bride, but with you-know-who coming, I want to look extra-special!"

"You are extra-special every day," Josie said as she sat up. "And, I've been a little distracted today, so I haven't been working as hard as I must've looked. I need to get more done before I go anywhere." Josie noted the cloud of disappointment roll across her best friend's face and was immediately sorry she had caused it. A thought came to her, and she shared it with Vikki. "How about you order us a couple of to-go sandwiches from Elroy's and we'll eat right here? We'll shut the door. I can hang out my 'Do not disturb' sign. I will give you my undivided attention for thirty minutes. That should provide a good release for me as well. What do you say?"

"Well . . . if that's all I get, I guess I'll have to take it!"

"Okay, then! Skedaddle until you bring me something to eat!" They both laughed, Vikki disappeared and Josie went back to work with a lighter heart.

What seemed like only moments later, Vikki was back, toting a pizza from the bar.

"Clear your desk this instant, boss, or you'll have pizza grease all over your work!" Vikki ordered, and then set the box down a spit-second after a spot was vacated. Then she drew two diet colas from her coat pockets, set them on the desk and threw her coat on the couch. She pulled up the folding chair and shut the door before sitting down. "Okay. I'm ready. Spill!"

"I'm sure I don't know what you mean," Josie demurred while twisting the cap off her soda pop. Then she pulled a cheesy slice from the box in front of her and shoved it into her mouth before Vikki could ask her a specific question. She couldn't very well talk with her mouth full, could she?

"So, what's the scoop on the New York bridal shower? Are we still going? Isn't that what your secret lunch was all about?"

Josie gave her a wide-eyed look and pressed her finger against her lips. "Shush!" she said through a mouthful of pizza. She glanced at the floor beneath the door to be sure there were no shadows lurking. Then she gulped down her mouthful before speaking in a whisper. "Yes. 'Hildy' will be attending the shower after all." Josie used her fingers to parenthesize Hildy's name. Then she quirked her eyebrows at Vikki.

"Ooh." Vikki said, raising her own eyebrows and nodding.

"Now, not another word about this unless we're at the park. Do you hear me?" Josie glared at Vikki until the other woman nodded her agreement. "With 'Hildy' along, everything should go smoothly." Josie winked and added, "You can't go wrong traveling with your personal attendant."

"Nope," Vikki said and filled her own mouth with a bite of pepperoni. Josie took a swig of her soda pop and was trying to think of something else to talk about when Vikki beat her to it. "So, have you decided on a style for your wedding dress? You've let this slide a little too long. Hopefully it won't need much tailoring."

"Not to worry. I got a note from Gen Eastland at the business incubator. She said her tailoring business is booming, but she would make time to take in my dress for me as a wedding present. She owns her own shop, you know, and was very pleased with the ads I designed for her. In return, she wants to do this for me."

"Oh, yeah! My mom had some suits fitted by Gen last fall." Vikki picked up another piece of pizza and ate heartily. She smiled at Josie and winked their little secret wink. Josie winked back and helped herself to a second piece of pizza also.

"I'll try to get the details worked out this weekend about our travel plans," Josie said when she had finished eating. "Let's go out to lunch on Monday and discuss them. Okay? Now, please take the rest of this out of here so I can get back to work." She smiled at Vikki to take the harshness out of the order.

"Will do, boss!" Vikki scooped up the box, closing it at the same time and grabbed her soda pop and coat and disappeared through the door.

Josie wiped her face with a tissue from the box on her desk, took a drink of her diet cola and replaced the cover. *I bet what Vikki really wanted was to talk about Andy!* Josie thought before picking up her charcoal and going back to work.

Ping! Josie's work computer told her she's got an email message. She clicked it open and read Vikki's note: *Don't think you're getting off the hook this easily, missy! You know I want to hear more about your FRIEND! I'm looking forward to having you reintroduce us! You'd better make that a New Year's Resolution.* ☺ *VLD*

LOL (laugh out loud), Josie typed back and closed out of email. *Hiring her may have been a mistake,* Josie thought, shaking her head. Yet she smiled as she went on to finish the ad in front of her. Vikki always made it fun to come to work. Josie just had to be the stronger one because she's the owner of the company. It was her responsibility to keep everyone on task. Monday couldn't come quickly enough for her either.

Chapter Nine
No Candy, Please

Josie got a call from Andy on Sunday evening. He just said he'd see her in New York. "Call me when you get into town. I'll meet you and your bridesmaids for lunch before you go to the Colesons," he had said. She agreed. They could go over the details at a neutral location that wouldn't be bugged.

Monday was another busy day at the office. Josie had sent Jessica out on location for a photo shoot. Hildy had gone with her to help with the videography, so Josie helped Vikki with answering the phones. They were able to alternate lunch times with Nathan so the office wouldn't be closed when they went to lunch.

"I had a hard time sleeping this weekend," Vikki said in an accusing tone. "I couldn't get that blond Adonis out of my head! When do I get to see him again?"

"Hold your horses! Let's get our burgers to go before we start making dates with Andy!" Josie said and leaned out of the car window to pay the man at the till. After he put her money in the till, he handed out their lunches. Josie took them and passed them on through to Vikki. Then Josie drove off toward the park. It may be winter, but like fashionable pumps, women often put up with unpleasant weather for the sheer prestige of the location.

Josie parked her Impala in the snow-covered parking lot and pulled on her earmuffs and gloves. Vikki slapped a stocking cap on her head and drew out a pair of mittens.

"How do you plan to eat with mittens on?" Josie asked.

"Never you mind," she huffed and got out of the car. When they had shut their doors, she turned toward Josie and confessed, "I lost my good driving gloves and can't afford to get another pair until pay day. Luckily I still had these from high school."

"Oh, yeah. They do look familiar, now that you mention it," Josie replied. When they had stepped a half dozen paces away from the car toward the abandoned shelter house, Josie caught Vikki by the arm.

"Andy called last night. He wants to meet us in New York for coffee as soon as we hit town."

"You mean he remembered me and want to see me?" Vikki's voice raised and her eyes grew wide with excitement.

"Nothing like that," Josie said, calmly shaking her head. "I think he wants to make sure you girls don't spill the beans when you see him dressed as Hildy."

"Oh, yeah. That's going to be hildy-larious!" Vikki attempted a joke. Josie smiled at her effort. Vikki snickered, sat at the picnic table and opened her McDonald's bag. She took out a regular cheeseburger and French Fries. She liked the value meals, especially the burgers with those delicately chopped onions. She chomped into it. Josie slid a fruit salad and Berry Parfait from her bag, along with bottled water, then opened her spork. Combining a spoon and a fork into one utensil really didn't make sense to Josie. How could one ever hope to eat soup with a spork? It was not a problem today, as she wasn't eating soup. So, she wiped the snow off the picnic seat, sat, and returned her attention to the topic at hand.

"This Hildy will go dress shopping and stay at P.J.'s parents with us, as well as attend the shower. 'She' must remain with us at all times, maybe even in the ladies restroom!"

"E-ew. That could be tricky!" Vikki exclaimed and pigged out on French fries.

Josie looked around the snow-clad park and shivered. It was beautiful and sad at the same time. Winter skies and lack of green grass and leaves added a drab dimension that Josie had all but forgotten. Working in an office all day and traveling the winter streets in darkness both ways, didn't add any more luster to winter than what she was looking at this minute. Not even the snow sparkled.

"On a brighter note, pardon the pun; I want a sparkling white wedding dress with sequins and pearls. I want it to be chalk white, not off-white or cream." Josie sounded so adamant; Vikki leaned around to look into her face.

"Are you okay?" she asked her best friend.

"Oh, yes!" Josie snapped her head around. "I was just noticing how gloomy it is out here. Not even the snow shines!"

"That's too bad, too," Vikki added. "I've always wanted an outdoor winter wedding. But, I would make sure there was plenty of light to make the snow sparkle like my eyes." She practically cooed when she talked about her eyes. They were the blackest black Josie had ever seen. "Anyway, Josie, what do you think P.J. will get you for Valentine's Day? Your favorite chocolates? Perfume? Red roses?"

"I told him no candy, please," Josie answered. "I explained that wedding dresses tend to run a size smaller than off-the-rack clothes. I didn't want to look like I had gained twenty pounds by having to put on a larger size dress. So, I'm cutting out sweets and salty snacks. No water retention for me, no sir! If I have to have the dress tailored, I want it taken in, not let out!"

"Did you decide on that off-the shoulder style with the full skirt, or the one with the sweetheart neckline and the fitted, straight skirt?" Vikki asked eagerly.

"I was up all night looking at the two online," Josie said, dragging it out a little. "I debated and debated, and finally said a prayer and slept on it."

"Alright, already! Out with it! Which one did you choose?"

"The straight skirted one with the gorgeous sweetheart neckline, of course!" Josie laughed. She was so happy. "I can't wait to try it on when we get to the Big Apple! Oh, say! It's time we headed back. I think my caramel frappe is now iced coffee!"

"So am I!" Vikki shouted and packed up their trash.

The two made their way back to the car, and to work.

< * >

On Valentine's Day, P.J. picked Josie up at her home after work. He was taking her to dinner. He was waiting for her in the family living room, visiting with Eleanor.

"What are you doing this evening?" he asked his future grandmother-in-law. "If you don't have any plans, I'm sure Josie won't mind if you join us."

"Ever the gentleman, you are!" Eleanor exclaimed and patted her red velvet vest over her heart. "Thank you, but no. I will be going over to the apartment building and playing cards with my new neighbors. I'm home now because I wanted to see Josie in her Valentine dress. I'll take your picture when she comes down. I also wanted to ask if you'd help me move into my new place this weekend. I have rented a small U-Haul truck. I think you'll be able to handle it. I also need a little muscle to get my bedroom set loaded. I don't suppose you have any friends from work that could give you a hand? I'll pay you all of course, and feed you lunch!"

"Yes, I can drive the truck for you, and I'll check at work tomorrow for some help. I'll bet my boss, Mr. Williams, would help, if he's not busy."

"Great! And, I'm going to ask Sid Silverstein tonight. He's coming to play cards with us, too." Eleanor seemed to blush.

"That's very nice," P.J. said. "Do you think he's bringing you some Valentine candy?"

"Oh, golly, no!" Eleanor said, turning bright red.

"Who's bringing Grams candy?" Josie asked as she floated into the living room.

"No one, dear! I just told P.J. Sid was playing cards with us tonight. He jumped to conclusions! Oh, my aren't you beautiful! Here, let me get the camera." She stood and picked up the camera from the end table. P.J. stood as well, an appreciative grin on his face. He walked over to Josie, drew her into his arms, and gave her a long, passionate kiss. Her heart raced and blood pounded in her ears.

"You look fabulous in your navy suit, too!" Josie said. "I've really liked seeing you in that suit! I remember seeing it the first time when you took me to Jes' and Jimmy's wedding."

"Well, if your New Year's Eve dress was sapphire, I guess you would call this one ruby, right?" P.J. asked. Josie nodded. "I really like that dress." Josie just smiled. She wasn't about to give it away that her wedding dress was very similar to this dress, with a sweetheart neckline.

"P.J. put your arm around Josie and look this way. Say cheese!" Eleanor snapped their picture. "Okay, you two run off and have a great evening, and, Happy Valentine's Day!"

"Happy Valentine's Day to you, too, Grams!" Josie said and kissed her grandmother before stepping out into the dark night. Josie was glad there were no stars tonight. A cloud cover would help keep the earth warmer than without it.

Chapter Ten
Moving Grams

Finally Eleanor's apartment was ready to move into and P.J. had arrange for his best man and two men from work to help move Gram's bedroom set, kitchen set and her personal belongings. The weather, while sunny, was bitter cold. Snow crunched underfoot and had to be shoveled before anything left the stately Victorian. P.J. labored for an hour clearing the steps and sidewalk before his friends arrived at 10 a.m.

"Come in and have some hot chocolate before you get to moving," Josie invited. P.J. stamped out his shovel and set it against the house and took the broom Josie handed him to brush the white powder from his boots and pant legs. "Turn around and I'll get your back and shoulders," Josie offered. Then the two proceeded into the hallway where P.J. left his boots and coat spread out to dry.

Just then the doorbell rang and Josie greeted Stan Baker, Jake Williams and Biff Bradshaw. She said, "Thank you so much for volunteering to help move Grams. Let me take your coats and you may go on down the hall to the kitchen and have some hot chocolate with P.J."

P.J. introduced his friends and supervisor to Eleanor, who instructed them to take a seat at the table while she poured.

"I also have a variety of teas and could perk up some coffee if you like," Eleanor said.

"No, thank you. Hot chocolate's fine," everyone said.

"So, how much are we moving? And, where's the U-Haul?" Mr. Williams asked.

"My bedroom set, from upstairs; it's stripped, emptied and ready to go," Eleanor said. "This kitchen set will be going, too. There's a recliner in the family room I want to take and the end table next to it. I had a hide-a-bed delivered earlier this week, so you boys don't have to break your backs over that heavy thing. The U-Haul should be here any minute now. It was supposed to be delivered."

As if on cue the doorbell rang again.

"I'll get it," Josie said and left the kitchen. She padded down the hall in her bedroom slippers, jeans and powder blue ski sweater. She opened the door, expecting a truck driver with a set of keys, but found a uniformed delivery woman whose hat said *Western Union*.

"Are you Josie Buchannon?" The woman asked without missing a beat.

"Yes. How may I help you?"

"I have a telegram here for you. Please sign on the line next to number 13." Josie did as she was asked and took the brown envelope the woman handed her.

"Thank you," the delivery woman said and spun on her heel to leave. Josie closed the door behind her, stunned into silence."

Josie turned the envelope over and tore it open. The one line message was enough to drain the blood from her face. It read:

REMEMBER THE WARNINGS I SENT YOU ABOUT NYC.

P.J. came down the hall to see what was taking Josie so long. He asked, "What's that?"

Without saying a word, Josie handed him the telegram, which he read silently.

"That bastard!" P.J. said in a stage whisper. He slapped the intrusive message against his thigh for emphasis. "Wait, just wait until we catch up to this stinker. I'll make him wish he had never set eyes on you!"

"How do you know it's a male?" Josie asked, forcing a smile to lighten the mood.

"I don't. Not for sure. But, don't women like to practice different styles of penmanship? Guys take the easy way out, cutting letters from a magazine or newspaper, sending telegrams . . ." He lifted the one in his hand high in the air and waived it, then gave it back to Josie. "Well, you'd better get this down to the police station. I don't know what you're going to tell your grandmother, but you'd better think of it fast!"

"Okay. How about the truck driver forgot enough bungee cords and you sent me to get some while you guys load the truck?"

"That should work. By the time we figure out we don't need them, you will have been to the police station already. Go for it." He said and went back to the kitchen while Josie slipped on her coat and boots, grabbed her purse and slipped out the front door.

Josie keyed the remote start so that the Impala had a chance to turn over a couple of times before she got in and left the driveway. She knew she should have warmed up the car properly, but if she went back into the kitchen to spend those minutes with everyone else, she was afraid her grandmother would suspect something was wrong. Josie couldn't afford that. Grams would pump her like a well-oiled pump and everything would come pouring out. She couldn't afford that. Josie drove slowly and carefully downtown to the police station because the roads were snow covered and slick. It was all she could do to keep the speedometer under 40 mph, though, as she really wanted to get this over with.

Finally, she pulled into the parking lot at the city building and rushed into the police station. Stopping at the front desk to request Sgt. Rodriguez, she was told to take a seat; the sergeant would be out momentarily.

"You're lucky I'm here," Rodriguez said as she ushered Josie into their usual conference room. "This was supposed to be my weekend off, but Officer Adams got sick. What's up?"

Josie pulled the evidence from her purse where she had stuffed it on the way out of her house and handed it to Sgt. Rodriguez. Rodriguez removed it from the envelope and scanned the message.

"Hmm. It's another warning from your mystery person. It must be closer to the time you are planning to go to the Big Apple, huh? This perp seems to be getting a little antsy," the sergeant said and put the telegram back into the envelope. "Who has seen this and how many of them have handled it?"

"Just my fiancé and I have touched it."

"Good. I'll send it down to the lab to see if they can lift any fingerprints, but it was likely dictated in person or called in. People sending telegrams don't normally come in contact with the actual product. I'll ask around at Western Union to see what they know about the sender. Thanks for bringing it in. I'll keep Agent Hoverstein informed for you."

Josie thanked the officer and high-tailed back to the house. By then the guys had the bedroom items loaded and were nearly done with the kitchen set. Josie grabbed the last chair and headed out to the U-Haul. Grams was bringing the end table and two men from Lakewood Technologies went back for the recliner.

"Grams and I will follow in my car," Josie said and waived at the three helpers. P.J. gave her a quick peck on the lips before jumping into the driver's seat of the U-Haul truck. The other guys piled in beside him on the bench seat.

"See you there!" he called and drove off.

Josie helped Eleanor over to the car and shut the door behind her. She almost skated around to the drive's side and slipped on a patch of ice as she tried getting into the car.

"Oh! Are you alright?" Eleanor asked, reaching across the driver's seat to try to grab Josie by the arm. Her reach ran short, so she dropped her useless hands into her lap. Her brow was furrowed in concern.

"I'm fine, Grams," Josie said, disgusted with herself for not paying more attention to the slippery cement. "I guess my mind was elsewhere." She started the ignition and backed out of the driveway for the second time that morning.

"What's the problem?" Eleanor asked. "I didn't see you give P.J. any bungee cords, so I know you didn't really go anywhere to get any. Where did you go? Did it have something to do with why you and P.J. took so long in the hall earlier? You're not planning a housewarming party for me for this afternoon are you? I won't be ready to entertain for a couple of weeks, yet."

"It's nothing like that, Grams," Josie said, biting her lower lip.

"There were actually two doorbell chines, weren't there? One was obviously the U-Haul delivery person, but who was the other one?"

"I am not at liberty to discuss this right now, Grams," Josie said in a pleading tone. "Please forgive me for keeping a secret. I'll share it with you soon, but not right this second, not here. Please?"

"Well, I suppose you know best, Josie girl," her grandmother said and sighed. "Tell me this, has there been another murder?"

"No." Josie said, hoping it was true and that it would remain true. They drove on in silence. Josie's stomach was tied in knots because she didn't like keeping secrets from Grams. But Andy said to tell no one else. Now, what was she going to do?

Chapter Eleven
The Big Spiced Apple

Gerald Sloan was the co-owner of Garvey, Sloan and Associates, LTD, but sometimes he felt like a figurehead. His wife, Louise, managed the telemarketing division and supposedly reported directly to him. However, there were times like today when he felt she outranked him somehow. Mrs. Sloan had left a note on his desk for him, which wouldn't have been that unusual, but she preferred to look him up in person and speak face-to-face.

"I have to talk to people over the phone all day long, most of them disgruntled customers who call in asking for a manager to speak with," Louise once stated. "I would prefer to converse with my husband, at least, in person." However, that wasn't always convenient, what with their various meetings and conferences that cluttered their schedules.

Today's note was typed presumably on her work computer as they had had breakfast together. The note read:

"Dear Gerald, I know this is sudden notice, but I have had an excessively stressful week, today in particular, and I need to go to the spa for the weekend. I have a migraine and will be taking a taxi. Please do not try to contact me as I will not be taking any calls. Love, Louise."

Louise had gone to a spa a few times in the past, not as suddenly as this, Gerald knew, but it wasn't too out of character for her, so he slid the note inside his middle desk drawer thinking he would deal with it later.

"Ah! She forgot about the shower Darlene Coleson is giving for Josie Buchannon tomorrow!" Sloan slapped his forehead. "If there's not a gift at home, I'll have to get one and send it with Darlene. Oh, what the heck!" He punched the intercom button on his telephone set, saying, "Pricilla! Come in here, please!"

"Yes, Mr. Sloan. How can I help you?" Pricilla asked as she entered the office. She wore her skirt a little too short for Mr. Sloan's taste and her heels were much too high. At one time, Mr. Sloan had even asked her to sign a safety waiver because of his fear she would fall off those 'stilts' and break her neck. He ignored that for the moment so he could get right to the reason he had summoned her.

"My wife had to take an unexpected trip and won't be here for Josie Buchannon's shower tomorrow. Would you please run out and get a bridal shower gift from Mrs. Sloan and me? Take the corporate credit card and buy her something nice, but for less than $100, okay?"

"Yes, sir, Mr. Sloan. Right way, sir!" Pricilla said and left.

< * >

Meanwhile, Josie had closed the office for the afternoon so that she and her bridesmaids could make it to the big city before a snowstorm hit. She didn't want to be driving in it, especially in the dark. She would pick up her staff at their respective homes, she no longer had to stop at the designated coffee shop to pick up Andy as he decided to come to her house. They would arrive at the Colesons' home in time for supper. That gave everyone a full evening to get acquainted.

It's a good thing Grams is living at the Silver Seasons Senior Apartments and wouldn't see Andy in his undercover costume. She would know in an instant it wasn't Hildy, Josie thought as she parked in the street in front of her house. *Just think, in a couple of months P.J. will be living here, too!* Josie's heart beat faster just thinking about it. She got out of the car and went inside to wait for Andy.

She no more than got inside and took off her coat when the doorbell rang. She answered the door to find a tall, stocky blond standing on the doorstep.

"Hi, Josie!" she heard in a falsetto voice. Josie giggled. "Andy?"

"No, dear. Hildy." He said and glided into the hallway. He pirouetted in front of her like a model. "How do you like my new ski bunny jacket? And aren't these fashion boots to die for?"

"Yes, they are!" Josie agreed. She pulled on her parka again and led Andy as Hildy out the front door, which she locked, and directed him to pull his Chevy Silverado into the garage where it would stay warm and dry over the weekend. It would be a tight squeeze with five females and their suitcases packed into Josie's Impala, but the bridesmaids, themselves, wanted it that way. And, Andy agreed that it would seem more natural to outsiders. But then came the moment of truth. As they picked up each bridesmaid, Andy swore them to secrecy, explaining his role in the bridal party and about the case. He also said that when they reached New York City, he would take over the driving. This could easily be explained as he was the personal attendant just doing her job.

"If any of you are afraid for your life, we can drop you back home before leaving town," Andy suggested as he'd finished explaining the situation with the threatening messages and his undercover role. "No one will fault you if that is what you decide. We can just tell Mrs. Coleson the weather scared you out."

"Oh, no! I wouldn't miss this for the world!' Vikki was the first to jump on board with the idea of being a part of the operation. Andy looked from her to Jessica, to Donna. Each one had wide eyes and were nodding in agreement. "We're all going," they said.

Along the road, Josie received a text from P.J., saying: *Change of plans. Surprise bachelor party keeps me in Lakewood. Sorry.* Josie was driving and didn't get it until later.

The ladies spent the entire road trip trying to talk all at once, excited about the weekend in the Big Apple and about the undercover investigation. Josie knew it wasn't the smartest thing to tell all these people about the situation, but how else would they pull it off that Andy was Hildy? It wouldn't look good for the bride to show up with a man who wasn't her fiancé even if he was her body guard. *God, please let this work*! Josie prayed.

It started snowing halfway to New York City. The girls stopped chatting so loudly in order that Josie could concentrate on driving. By the time they arrived at the Colesons', their speed had dropped to 35 mph.

"Good thing we left early!" Vikki said as she exited the car. She was always the optimist. "I'm glad we made it!" She turned around and gave Andy a hug.

"Oof!" Andy said, having been surprised by the bear hug. "Look out, dear! Everyone will think we're a couple!"

"Well, we're in the Big Apple, who's going to care? And, we know the truth," Josie overhead Vikki whisper to Andy.

"Stop flirting, you two! Everybody, grab some luggage!" Josie yelled as she opened the trunk. Parka sleeves rubbed wool coat sleeves as the gals rushed to obey. Mrs. Coleson opened the front door wide as the visitors approached.

"Just stomp off the snow as you go. The staircase is just down the hall," she directed. "Welcome everyone! I'm so glad you all could make it!"

After squaring everyone away, much as Josie had anticipated—keeping Andy to himself in the den—Mrs. Coleson seated the company around the dining room table as she put the finishing touches on their evening meal. The house phone rang and she brought it into the dining room and handed it to Josie. Josie's face scrunched up in an inquisitive look.

"Is it Grams? Is something wrong?" she asked Mrs. Coleson while covering the mouthpiece. Mrs. Coleson simply shook her head and raised her shoulders.

"He wouldn't say," she whispered back.

"Hello?" Josie said into the receiver. "Who is this?"

"Just a reminder that I warned you something bad will happen if you come to New York," a muffled voice said. "I have one and will take another hostage if you go to that shower." Click. The caller had hung up. Josie put the phone down and looked at Hildy, her eyes wide in fear.

Chapter Twelve
Bridal Surprises

Andy, as Hildy, stood and took the phone away from Josie and guided her out of the Colesons' dining room.

"We'll be right back," he called over his shoulder in his Hildy voice. "Just some girl talk. Go ahead and talk amongst yourselves!" He guided Josie all the way upstairs to the twins' bedroom and shut the door. "Okay, what did you hear?"

"The voice was muffled, but it said the person has taken a hostage!" Josie said and dropped onto the bed. "Not only that, but he said he'd take another hostage if I go to the shower tomorrow.

"I have to call Grams!" Josie said and pulled her cellphone out of her pocket. She dialed Eleanor's new telephone number and was relieved to hear her grandmother's voice on the other end. Her sigh of relief startled her grandmother.

"What is it pussycat?" Eleanor asked. "I can hear the concern in your voice. Does it have to do with that secret you've been keeping?"

"Yes, Grams," Josie said and saw Andy shaking his head so violently his wig nearly fell off. "I mean, no, Grams. I just wanted to let you know we made it here safe and sound, and I hope that you are enjoying your new apartment." Andy was nodding his approval. He patted her shoulder for emphasis. "Well, Darlene is putting supper on the table. I'd better go. Just take care, okay? Love you! Bye!"

"Good cover," Andy said softly. "Yes, we should get back downstairs before Vikki or someone else comes up."

"Wait!" Josie grabbed the sleeve of Andy's plus-size silk jacket. "We should call the Lakewood Police and ask them to send someone over to protect Grams. Please call them!"

"You're right again." Andy pulled out his own cell phone and speed dialed the Lakewood Police Department. Asking for Sgt. Rodriguez, he quickly put in the request and hung up. "Happy now?"

"Yes. And starved. Let's go!"

Downstairs, the dining room table was brimming with aromatic scents that tantalized Josie's senses. Sitting, she looked around at all the beaming faces and the steaming pot of beef stew. There was a basket of fresh dinner rolls and three pies of various flavors. Darlene had put on a great spread.

"It's about time you got down here!" Patti shouted unnecessarily since she and her sister were seated on either side of Josie. "I don't know how much longer I could wait to eat!"

"And, we wanted to give you a gift for your personal shower now since we weren't able to make it up to Lakewood for it," Pauline added, giving her twin a nasty look and mouthed, *You pig*! She pulled up a wrapped gift from its hiding place in her lap and handed to Josie.

"Why, thank you! You really didn't have to, especially with hosting your own shower tomorrow," Josie said, smiling and accepting the package. She pulled off the white curling ribbon and carefully slit through the clear tape holding the baby blue gift wrap on the present. Inside she found a bath and shower gel set with a coordinating scented candle and a small gift card. Josie held up the gift for everyone to see and then hugged the girls. She said, "Ooh! This is very nice! I'll enjoy it very much. Thank you!"

"Read the card aloud!" Patti exclaimed and covered a snicker with her hand. Pauline's face and ears turned beet red. Josie picked up the card and opened it.

"It says, 'May you and P.J. have hours and hours of good clean fun!'" Josie raised her eyebrows at the girls, but couldn't help but smile.

"Let's eat before it gets cold," Darlene interrupted. "How about everyone holds hands for the dinner prayer?" She led them through it.

"Where's Mr. Coleson?" Vikki wanted to know.

"He went to Lakewood to stay with P.J. for the weekend," Darlene said.

"Yeah, the groomsmen are throwing him a bachelorette party!" Patti said, looking smug. "I bet Stan got a huge cake with a girl in a bikini jumping out."

"I hope he has more brains than that!" Pauline replied.

"So, it's just 'us girls' for the weekend! How nice," Andy said in his Hildy voice, and fluttered his mascaraed eyelashes. "Maybe we could paint our toenails tonight."

Josie and Vikki choked on their stew. The other women nodded and the twins cheered.

< * >

The next morning, the girls followed a suggested bathroom schedule laid out for them by Mrs. Coleson the night before. Everything ran in an orderly fashion and they were out the door in record time. Since the bridal shower at GS&A wasn't until 2:30 p.m., they piled into two vehicles and headed downtown to David's Bridal for a look at bridesmaids' dresses, picking up breakfast sandwiches and coffee to go at a fast food place along the way.

"Why don't you each pick out a modestly priced gown and model it," Josie suggested. "Then we'll vote on the one we all like best. If there is a tie, I will be the tiebreaker. You all know my main color is powder blue, so be sure the style you pick comes in that color. If you forget, come look at this suit I'm wearing." Then she let them loose on the store while she went to the accessories section to look at shoes and veils.

As she was looking at her reflection in the mirror wearing a tiara headpiece, her cellphone signaled an incoming text message. She flipped it open and read:

NOW 2 WOMEN WILL MISS YOUR SHOWER.

Fear gripped Josie's heart, freezing her in her tracks for moments that seemed like an eternity. She shook her head to clear it and the tiara fell into her hands, on top of her phone. Carefully, she set the crown back on the shelf and refocused on the text. She hit forward and sent it to Andy, then she sank onto the satin cushioned bench next to her. A moment later and Andy was by her side, putting his arm around her shoulders.

"I don't know how long I can go on with this!" Josie whispered. "He's not after me, physically, but now I'm responsible for two missing people!"

"Hold on, we don't know that he's taken anyone, just yet. Text your bridesmaids and tell them to hurry. The more we stay together the safer they'll be. I'll phone this in." He pulled out his cellphone, forwarded the menacing message to headquarters, and then dialed to speak with his supervisor. Josie had managed to hear back 'K' from all her party except Patti. *Now what?* Josie thought. *The kidnapper had better not have gotten her, too!*

Just then, Patti came prancing up to her, twirling in a hot pink number with a short front hemline and longer in back. The others followed her, including Mrs. Coleson. Josie heaved a sigh of relief.

"I'm glad you could all work so quickly and responded when I texted," Josie glared at Patti. "Most of you that is. So, let's see what you have."

"Sorry!" Patti replied. "I was already on my way back here, so I didn't think it mattered. But, look what I found! Don't you just love this cool hemline?" She twirled again and struck a pose.

"Does it come in powder blue?" Josie asked, her eyes trying to focus on the design and her hand reaching out to feel the material. Josie struggled to keep her mind on the dress in front of her and not on the big questions looming in the back of her mind: Who has been kidnapped?

"Yes, it does! And I love the halter top!" Patti answered. She bent over, Marilyn Monroe-style and exposed some cleavage Josie hadn't realize she had developed until now.

"I think we can find something less revealing," Mrs. Coleson interjected and pushed Patti into an upright position.

"Like this?" Pauline asked and pirouetted onto the pedestal. She was wearing a petal-soft pink floor-length dress with a ruffled turtleneck and a full flounce. She extended her arms, fully covered with Victorian lace sleeves and a wide zippered cuff.

"Better," Josie said, and got an elbow in the ribs from Vikki. "Who's next?"

Vikki bounced up and paraded in front of the mirror and everyone in attendance. She narrated her own modeling, "Note the fitted princess seaming, the slit half sleeves, very flattering to all arms," at which Pauline poked Patti in the back of her fleshy upper arm. "It has a v-neckline, but not too low. Notice the tulip hem. As you can see, it comes in the requisite powder blue. And this satin ribbon for a self-tie belt is detachable." She strutted around the wedding party and lingered in front of Andy.

Josie cleared her throat to warn Vikki not to get to into flirting with Andy while he was undercover. "Very nice, that's definitely worth considering. Donna, what did you find?"

Donna had gone all out on her Goth look that morning. The black lipstick and heavy eyeliner had been somewhat complimentary to the red leather mini skirt and black lace top she had brought along for the shower, but was a distraction when it came to wearing powder blue. The dress she had selected was the right color, but also sported an above-the-knee hemline. The satin gown had a mandarin collar with a keyhole peephole immediately beneath it, and the waste line was much too fitted for some of the more fuller-figured bridesmaids. Donna just stood there with her hands on her waist.

"Okay, good color," Josie, ventured. "Jessica, how about you? You're the model at work, what did you discover?"

"I found this lovely frock that really rocks!" Jessica gently pushed Patti off the pedestal and slowly turned around like a music box dancer. With her cocoa coloring, the shiny bronze material really made her ebony eyes sparkle. The sleeveless sheath had a ruffled v-neckline and a ruffled floor-length hemline that extended up the slit in front of the left leg.

"It's a knockout," Josie said, while the others oohed and ahed. "But does it come in powder blue and doesn't that ruffle make it hard to walk in?"

"You texted me while I was trying it on, and I didn't have a chance to ask if it came in powder blue. Sorry."

"Let me see the tag," Mrs. Coleson said as a bridal consultant stepped up to assist.

"Tangerine and spice, besides the bronze," the consultant stated. "Isn't it beautiful?"

"It's stunning, but not quite my taste," Josie said. "I'm the bride and my colors are powder blue, navy and white. So, I guess that one is ruled out. Sorry, Jes!"

Everyone turned toward Andy. Jes raised her eyebrow and discreetly pointed to her phone, which was still out. Andy slightly shook his head. Glancing around, he realized the others were wondering what Hildy had found.

"I'm sorry," he said in his Hildy voice. "Nothing I looked at appealed to me. However, I believe Vikki came up with a winner. I vote for her choice of gown." Vikki preened and nearly purred her happiness that he would pick her dress.

"I think the girls would all look great in that one as well," Mrs. Coleson said. "And, since I'm paying for my girls' dresses, I vote for that one on their behalf."

"Aw, Mom!" Patti complained.

"It could have been worse," Pauline said. "I'm fine with that one."

"Me, too," Jess added, and stepped off the pedestal.

"It's not very bold, but I'd be the only hold-out, so I guess I'll go with the flow," Donna said.

"Great!" Josie said. "Let the consultant take your measurements and we're done here."

The girls left for the dressing rooms along with Mrs. Coleson and the bridal consultant. That left Andy and Josie sitting on the bench alone.

"I'm just the personal attendant, right? I don't need to get measured, correct?" Andy asked, concern shadowing his woman's voice.

"That's right, 'Hildy'," Josie reassured him. "And, I promised 'you', you could wear a slack outfit if you really wanted to." Josie patted Andy on the shoulder and then looked him in the eye. "Just what's going on? Who's going to miss my bridal shower?"

"The bureau has a list of prospective victims including your bridesmaids," Andy said, "Let's go wait by the dressing rooms to keep a better eye on the girls, just in case."

As they walked, Andy's phone buzzed. "Hello?" He listened for a minute and hung up, his lips pressed tightly closed. "Mrs. Garvey has gone missing. And, Mrs. Sloan is supposed to be at a spa, but didn't leave any contact information."

Josie gasped.

Chapter Thirteen
The Show Must Go On

Andy took Josie's elbow to calm her. Two women were missing. The wives of Josie's former bosses at Garvey, Sloan and Associates, LTD were not bridal party members, but they were friends of hers and should have been honored guests at the shower hosted at their husbands' office building. Josie was beside herself with fear and anxiety.

"Hold it together," Andy said. "We can't let the others know about this, not yet. We have to go through with this charade. My supervisor has agents out combing New York to find these women, starting with spas, in case they really did go there, hopefully together. Until then, the show must go on, as they say. Got it?"

Just then the dressing room curtains parted to reveal most of the bridal party in the clothes they had arrived. Mrs.

Coleson and the twins were still in the family size cubicle with the consultant. Vikki took one look at Josie's blank expression and knew something was wrong.

"What's up?" she whispered, drawing close to her best friend. "And, don't say, 'Nothing'." She squeezed Josie's forearm to enforce her demand.

"Later," was all Josie could muster. To everyone, she said, "Don't forget your coats! It's cold outside!" *Oh, that was lame*, Josie, she thought to herself. *Of course it's cold outside; it's New York in the dead of winter! Now I know I'm upset; I can't even say anything intelligent!*

Josie felt pressure on both her arms as Andy and Vikki each gave her a supportive hug. Sometimes it was like Vikki could read her mind, and now, Andy too seemed to know how she was feeling. *Maybe playing a woman all weekend has blessed him with some feminine intuition.* Josie's belly jerked with a suppressed chuckle. *They'll all think I'm crazy if I start laughing now,* Josie thought, *but maybe a little levity is just what the doctor would order.* She watched as her bridesmaids lined up to pay for their orders and then put on their coats. Then Andy and Mrs. Coleson herded the girls to the parked cars like mother hens with their chicks.

Soon, they had arrived at the parking lot of GS&A and Josie and Mrs. Coleson were leading a guided tour through the building and up the elevator, which was filled to capacity with just their party. The group entered the board room where it was evident a party was about to take place. The tables were pushed into a horseshoe shape, draped with light blue plastic table clothes with white bells hanging from the edges. There were side tables, one piled with wrapped presents and another filled with refreshments, all kinds of bars, punch and coffee. Several women whom Josie had met while she worked here were already seated at the horse shoe table setting. They looked up as Josie and her crew walked in and waved. Some called, "Hi, Josie!"

Mrs. Coleson led the party around to the top of the horse shoe and took their coats from them.

"Have a seat," she said and went to hang up their outerwear on the coatrack in the corner of the room. When she came back, she spoke quietly, but still loud enough for Josie and her daughters to hear. "I need to run to my desk for my reading for the shower. If I'm late, I've asked Bridgette Saunders, there in the long red hair, to be the mistress of ceremonies. She'll keep the ball rolling. I'll be right back. Just stay put." She smiled, hugged Josie and took her leave.

Five minutes later, precisely at 2:30 p.m., Bridgette rose and smiled toward the head table.

"Good afternoon!" she said in a commanding voice. She obviously didn't need a microphone to project her voice over the din in this room. "I'm Bridgette Saunders, your Emcee for today. I want to welcome you all to the bridal shower of Josie Buchannon, bride-to-be of P.J. Coleson, Darlene Coleson's son. You all know Darlene, even if you don't know me. Darlene had to step out a moment, but she will be right back. She said to 'Get this party started!' So that's just what we're going to do. Starting with head table introductions. Josie, would you please stand up with your bridal party? Thank you! And, yes, there's going to be a quiz on what you learn about these women, so listen closely! Bridesmaids, as Josie calls your name, please raise your hand and tell us briefly your name, where you live and how you know Josie and for how long. Thanks! Great! Let's get started!"

Josie took the cue, began with her BFF and maid of honor, Vikki, and worked her way down to the end, with her personal attendant, Hildy. Luckily, Andy had worked for Sanders & Sons briefly the previous year, undercover as their night janitor, so he got to know things about the staff that even they weren't aware of. This fact helped him pass the pop quiz that was set before him. The audience clapped as loudly for him, as Hildy, as they had for the rest of the bridal party. Then Bridgette invited them to sit down again, and turned to the audience.

"On the papers in front of you, I want you to number your papers from one to seven. Starting on this end, correspond the numbers to the members of the bridal party. After each number, write three things you remember each of them saying. You may include their names as one of the items. This will be a timed event. You have 60 seconds. Go! The person with the most right answers wins a free can of soda pop to take home!"

Twenty minutes later the game came to a hilarious ending as one of the women in the audience shared some mistaken 'facts' about Hildy. The soda pop was awarded to Sonja Johnson whom Josie remembered from data processing. Josie started watching the door with brief glances at Andy. Darlene hadn't returned yet, and Josie was getting a creepy feeling at the base of her neck. Whenever she caught Andy's eye, though, he would either tap his finger on his lips or just smile sweetly. I guess that's his way of saying, 'Just be patient', Josie thought. She looked down at her twiddling thumbs in her lap and said a silent prayer that Darlene was okay and on her way back to the conference room. Then she plastered a smile on her own face and looked up at Bridgette, hoping she had another stimulating game to play.

Bridgette was busy setting up music on a piano she must have had brought in for the occasion. Josie didn't remember ever having seen a piano in the room before. This one was a small, brown spinet that most people pushed up against their living room walls and left to the dust.

"In your programs is a cute little love song I wrote for the occasion. It's to the tune of Mary Me, Molly, so I called it Mary Me, Josie. Please turn to it and sing along." She started the introduction to the song, which was actually a familiar tune, so Josie had fun singing about P.J.'s and her budding romance. Darlene must have filled Bridgette in on the details of how they met. Even P.J.'s proposal at the Country Music fest was in the song. Josie couldn't help smiling as she sang as the little ditty brought back some very fond memories.

When the song was over, Josie noticed that Bridgette's eyes had started going to the door more frequently as well. Darlene still wasn't back. Bridgette had to move passed Darlene's spot in the program and introduce the next poet. Kathy Crandall, who took over the accounting job Josie vacated to go home and help the FBI, stood and read a love poem she had written. It had the right number of syllables in each line, and it rhymed, but it was obviously the work of an amateur and had more to do with her own love desires than it did P.J.'s and Josie's. But everyone clapped politely, acknowledging her effort.

Finally, Bridgette turned the program over to Josie to open presents while she went to the dessert table to check on refreshments. Josie handed the scissor to Andy, knowing he'd be cool under this pressure and not cut himself as she was afraid she'd do to herself if she kept them. The bridal party formed an assembly line and made swift work of the pile of presents and sent the opened boxes down one side of the horse shoe and up the other so everyone could see what she got. When the last one left her hands, Josie stood to give her thank-you speech.

"I want to thank you all for coming today," Josie began. "It's been a fun afternoon and I really appreciate all the gifts, cards and . . ."

"You missed one," Vikki said and handed her another card. "It had gotten stuck in the ribbon of that last gift. Sorry I hadn't noticed it before."

"Thanks, Vikki! Things like that happen!" Josie said brightly. She looked at the envelope, and looked again. Something about the handwriting looked familiar. Josie's stomach lurched. She thought it was just because she was hungry, and the last thing on the program was lunch. She rubbed her hand along the waistband of her powder blue skirt before opening the envelope and taking out the card. Josie caught herself before reading it aloud. It said:

HOPE YOU HAVE A HAPPY WEDDING WITHOUT YOUR MOTHER-IN-LAW!

"What?" Josie gasped. "I can't believe it! Here, Andy, I mean Hildy. Take care of this, please." To the wondering crowd, she said, "I can't believe all the nice things you all gave me. And, this card isn't from any of you, but it has a great effect on our wedding. If any of you are ever in Lakewood, I hope you drop by and visit us! Thanks! We have to go now."

As Josie and her bridal party picked up their purses and headed toward the coat rack, Bridgette retook command of the crowd. She thanked them all for coming again and assured Josie that she and Darlene would have the gifts delivered to the Coleson home for her. Josie thanked her and rushed out the door. Andy was on his phone as soon as he hit the hallway. He and Josie led the bridal party at a trot to the elevator. The girls were all hushed until the elevator doors shut them in, then they all began questioning Josie and Andy at once.

"Why did Josie call you 'Andy'?" the twins wanted to know.

"What's going on that you blew his cover?" Vikki demanded of Josie.

"Isn't Andy the FBI agent that was your night janitor last year?" Patti and Pauline asked simultaneously. Then they both turned to Vikki and said, "And, you knew about this?"

Andy reached out and slammed the Halt Elevator button. Everyone shut up then and stared at him. He said, "Yes, I'm Andy Hoverstein, FBI agent. Yes, I worked at Sanderson & Sons, undercover, last year, and I'm undercover again. Hildy couldn't make it this weekend, and didn't change her mind at the last minute. That was just a ruse to get me into the picture. Josie's been receiving threatening notes about kidnappings. We think Mrs. Coleson is the third in a series of kidnappings. Now, listen up! This is extremely crucial that you follow my instructions to the letter. First, Josie will drive you all back to the Colesons in Mrs. Coleson's van. You will lock the doors behind you once you are in the house. You will all stay together in the den where there are no windows and there's a bathroom where you should be safe. I will send an officer over to guard you. Do not let the officer in the house, at least not without confirming his or her name with me. I will call you with it later. You will not answer the telephone—just let the answering machine get it. Do you hear me?"

"What are you going to do?" Josie asked timidly.

"I'm going to stay behind and see if the kidnapper is still in the vicinity. If he is, he might just take some bait—a lone bridal party member. Don't worry, I'll call for backup," Andy said and punched the resume button to restart the elevator. Be as calm as you can while you go to the car. Josie, you can do this. I've seen how you've handled pressure. Just do as I said, okay?"

"Yes, sir," Josie answered. "I'd just feel better if you were going with us."

"This was part of the plan all along. Just stick to it. I'll call you later. Now go," he said as the elevator doors opened on the parking lot level. All the real females exited the elevator and headed toward the parked van, trying not to look suspicious. Andy called after them in his Hildy voice, "You ladies run along. I have to find the restroom. I'll bring Josie's car when I'm done. Ta ta!" He watched as they safely entered the van and left, then allowed the elevator doors close on him. He rode it to the main floor and got off, slowly making his way to the ladies' room, which was down a short hall.

Suddenly, a wiry arm snaked around his neck and he felt the sharp edge of a blade at his throat, just under his ear near his jugular vein. A gravelly voice whispered in his ear, "Don't move and you won't get hurt!" The arm around his neck slid back and so that the attached hand with a wet rag was able to cover his face. It reeked of ether. Andy struggled against the fumes, but they were too strong; they overpowered him. The darkness rolled in, and he dropped like a dead weight.

Chapter Fourteen
Fear Finds a Home

Josie drove her Impala instead of the Coleson van because she felt more confident in driving her own vehicle. The bridesmaid were stuffed like sardines in the five-seated vehicle. She gripped the steering wheel so tightly, her knuckles turned white.

"Patti, keep your head down!" Josie was nearly shouting. With only five seats in her car, Josie was forced to ask the athletic Patty to lie across the laps of Jessica, Donna and Pauline in the back. Patti accepted, finding it just the levity she needed at the moment. "We don't want to attract the attention of any cops on patrol. I don't want to get stopped. I don't want a ticket, but it's all I can do to keep from speeding. I don't need any other distractions, either. So, no,

Vikki! Please don't turn on the radio. You can listen to that at the Colesons' or turn on the television."

"Sheesh!" Vikki said with frustration shading her tone. "Calm down, sweetie, before you burst a blood vessel! I just wanted to see if there was anything on the news about those missing women. But, let's talk about something else then. What would take your mind off your future mother-in-law having gone missing?"

Josie shot Vikki a nasty look.

"Oops! Sorry, I shouldn't have said that either."

"Amazing grace, how sweet the sound," Jessica started singing. Pauline started sobbing. Jessica shut up.

"Let's play that license plate game!" Donna suggested. "There's one from Vermont! There's one from New York. Another from New York. Hmm, I guess most of them are from New York. Well, that was boring."

"I'd have played with you," Patti said, poking Jessica in the chest, "but I can't see anything from down here!" Donna grabbed her hand and guided it to her shoulder instead.

"I know, let's talk about the wedding rehearsal. That'll be at the church, right, Josie?" Vikki asked. "What kind of menu will be on the rehearsal dinner? Will that be at the church, too, or will it be at your house? If we're too many people, maybe you could rent the community center. The groom's parents pay for that, anyway, right? So, they'll . . . probably . . . decide . . . where . . . ?"

"You're not helping," Josie said, frowning at Vikki.

"You're right; I'm not very good at distractions. I'm sorry."

"Let's sing something campy, something funny!" Donna suggested. "How about Ninety-nine Bottles of Beer? Ninety-nine bottles of beer on the wall, ninety-nine bottles of beer!" Patti joined in, but everyone else groaned.

Just then, Josie pulled into the Coleson driveway and everyone piled out. Pauline had her house key ready and let everyone inside then locked the door from the inside.

"Everyone in the living room for a meeting!" Josie took control, herding the others into the general direction she wanted. She felt like a mother hen ushering her chicks into the brooder coop with her wings out to catch the strays. She almost chuckled. Almost. Patti plopped onto the area rug in front of the sofa. Pauline sat behind her and put her hand on her sister's shoulder. Jessica and Vikki joined her on the sofa. Donna flopped into the larger of the two recliners, which dwarfed her. A flash of Lilly Tomlin, in reruns of Laugh-In, rocking in a giant rocker came unbidden to Josie's mind. One thought led to another, reminding Josie she would have to call Grams when this meeting was adjourned.

"Alright," Josie said, drawing everyone's attention. "The situation isn't good. Our body guard has been called into action to find three women half of us know and love. It's up to us to stay strong and hold down the fort.

"The first order of business is to secure the premises. The second order will be to call home and relay the events—in as calm a voice as we possibly can. Then, the third order of business will be to stay together." Josie ticked off the list on her fingers as she spoke. "There are six of us. We will divide into groups of two to secure the premises. I don't want anyone going anywhere alone, not even to the bathroom. Do I make myself clear?"

"Yes." "Uh huh." "Got it!" "Okay." "I hear ya."

"Great. Now, Patti, I want you to take Donna with you to the basement and make sure all the windows are locked. On your way back, make sure to secure the basement door, somehow. Lock it, barricade it, whatever. Then high-tail it back here where you and Pauline can call your dad from your cell phone, not the house phone, okay? Go! Pauline, you take Jessica upstairs and do the same. If you're scared to go into the attic, just be sure that door is locked and slide a heavy chest of drawers in front of it. Stop by the bathroom and bring down more toilet tissue and any other items from the bedrooms, like blankets and pillows, that you think we could use. Any questions? Good! Hustle!

"Vikki, you and I will check all the doors and windows on this level, look for flashlights, candles and matches, things like that, and snacks. We'll bring it all back here for a slumber party . . . of sorts." Vikki just nodded and fell in behind Josie as she went around the room checking windows for locks and pulling drapes. Soon, everyone was back in the living room with supplies and cell phones.

"Before you dial, just remember not to talk too long. We don't want to drain the batteries and not have a phone to call the authorities if we need to," Josie advised.

"What about the house phone?" Pauline asked, holding up the receiver.

"If the kidnapper comes here, he will probably cut the telephone line before attempting to break into the house. That phone won't do us any good. Besides, it may be bugged. So, just keep your calls short. Then, we'll put in a movie or something to keep our minds off what's going on out there. Okay, ladies, call home!"

While the twins called their dad, Vikki called her parents and Jessica called her husband, Jimmy, Josie noticed Donna wasn't dialing. She made a mental note to talk to her about that, but first things first: she had to call P.J.

"Hi, honey! I'm so glad to hear from you!" P.J.'s voice came over the line. "I've been so worried about your trip; I haven't really enjoyed my bachelor's party."

"Hi, P.J.! I'm so glad to hear your voice. All is not well here, and I'm glad your dad is with you," Josie tried to ease into the announcement she dreaded making. "You guys will want to come home when you hear what has happened."

"What? Are the girls okay? What happened?"

"There have been three kidnappings that I know of and your mom was one of them." Josie winced as she pictured the shock on P.J.'s face. She opened her eyes and scratched her head.

"Did you say Mom was kidnapped? Or do we have a bad connection. Oh, wait, Dad's pulling my sleeve saying the same thing. Where are the twins?" His voice took on a rushed quality that indicated he was on the move.

"They're with me, Vikki, Jes and Donna at your folks' place. We've secured the entrances and collected campout supplies. We're staying together in the living room. I'll let you go so we can both conserve our cellphone batteries. I love you! Drive safely!"

"I love you, too, Josie! Stay put!" P.J. disconnected. *Now to call Grams*, Josie thought. Oh, she dreaded this call. She didn't want to scare her. *I'll have to edit the story some.*

"Hello, dear! How was the shower?" Grams' voice came over the line. Josie heaved a heavy sigh. At least Grams was okay.

"Oh, we're all okay, except P.J.'s mom is missing. Andy Hoverstein is looking for her, though," Josie rushed to put a positive spin on her story. "You remember him, right? He kept an eye on me last summer when we were trying to catch Cass."

"Yes, I remember him. He's a good agent. He'll find her," Grams agreed. "Just what happened?"

She would have to ask, Josie thought, frustrated. She yanked on her suit jacket. A powder blue button popped off. Eagle eye Vikki snatched it up and handed it back to Josie.

"Well, Grams, we think she may have been kidnapped. I got a note at the shower saying I shouldn't have come back to New York. So, I feel like it's all my fault," Josie said and sniffed back a tear.

"Now, don't go doing that, Josie, girl," her grandmother said sternly. "You've never done anyone wrong and should not have this laid in your lap. Do the authorities have any leads?"

"Just the note . . ." Josie almost said 'notes', but caught herself. That would be a dead give-away, and she wasn't ready to go into the whole story just yet. "Tell you what, Grams, when I get back home, I'll have all the facts for you. Right now, all I really know is I should get off the phone in order to save on battery. Okay? I love you. You stay safe, okay?"

"I love you, too, pussycat. You're the one who needs to stay safe, you and your bridesmaids."

Chapter Fifteen
Three for One

While the Josie and her bridesmaids huddled together it the Colesons' living room and P.J. and his father were on their way to New York City, Andy was coming to in a studio apartment not far from the GS&A building. His eyesight was blurry, and he tried to rub his eyes. His hands were tied with a man's necktie. He studied it and tried to untie it with his mouth. Instantly regretting it he spat on the floor. The tie had been laced with Numb-zit, a children's thumb-sucking deterrent. His eyes watered from the bitter treatment, eventually helping to clear up his vision to some extent.

Looking around the apartment, Andy spotted the three missing women sitting around the room on various chairs. Their hands were tied behind them, their legs tied to chair legs and gags in their mouths. Their eyes were glued to him. His hands went up to his hair to check his identity status. Whew! The wig had stayed in place. Those guys in the costume department really knew their stuff. At least his cover wasn't blown, thank goodness! Assessing his situation further, he noticed his legs were also tied together, but he was seated, actually lounging, on a sofa. Just as Andy tried to pull his gag out of his mouth, keys jangled in the hall and clicked in the lock.

The gangly man with shaggy hair that walked through the door wasn't familiar to Andy, but the women seemed to know him. They were trying to talk through their gags and imploring him or chiding him, Andy wasn't sure which. They didn't seem afraid of him, though, and this intrigued Andy.

The man walked over to Andy and gently pushed some of the hair from the wig out of his face.

"Hi, Hildy," he said softly. "I'm really sorry about having to tie you up. I couldn't risk you trying to run. You look strong enough to really give me a run for my money. I bet you'd be good in the sack because of your strength." He turned toward the other women and said. "I'm going to give you each a bathroom break; one at a time of course. Don't try anything funny. Don't remove your gag while you're in there. If you do try to escape or call out, I'll have to make you pee in a can out here where I can keep tabs on you. Mrs. Sloan, you were here first, you may go first. Just remember, I will also have a gun on these others, so don't do anything stupid."

He reached down and untied Mrs. Sloan's restraints, beginning with her ankles, and then helped her up. He escorted her to the bathroom and held the door partly open while she made her way over to the toilet. Stepping to one side to give her some privacy, he eyed the other women suspiciously. When his brooding eyes reached Hildy, they sparked a bit and moved on. Mrs. Sloan could be heard washing her hands, causing the kidnapper to swing the door open and take her by the elbow back to her assigned chair. He then turned his attention to the other two.

"Mrs. Garvey, you're up!" And, a few minutes later, it was Mrs. Coleson's turn.

When it came to Hildy's turn, the kidnapper used a gentler approach. He sat on the sofa and lifted her feet onto his lap to untie her restraints. When he stood, he put his arms around her waist and half lifted her to her feet.

"Come on, sweetheart," he practically cooed. "After the excitement of the day, I bet you really have to go. Let me help you." When they reached the door, he reached down and untied her hands as well. Andy was waiting for just such a break. It was all he could do to stand still until his captor finished untying the tainted necktie, but as soon as it was done, Andy cupped his captor's face almost affectionately with one hand, and punched him soundly with the other. The kidnapper never knew what hit him. He was down and out. Andy reached up and removed the neck tie that acted as his gag and then used it to tie up the kidnapper. He searched through the kidnapper's pockets and fished out his cellphone.

"Does anyone know where we are?" he asked in his own voice. Mrs. Coleson nodded, the other two shook their heads. All three had had eyebrows shooting off the tops of their heads. Andy walked over and untied Mrs. Coleson's gag, then her other bonds.

"That is Terry Richards," Mrs. Coleson said. "He works in the mail room for Garvey, Sloan and Associates. He lives within walking distance of work. This seems to be his apartment. I think it's in the Red Oak Apartments. We came up two flights of stairs, which must mean . . ."

"We're on the third floor, right!" Andy said. "You untie the other two while I check the door for an apartment number." As he walked to the door, he was dialing 9-11. He opened the door and reported the crime, including the location. When he returned, all three women where untied and rubbing their wrists, ankles and the sides of their faces. They turned to look at their liberator.

"Oh! Hi! I'm Andy Hoverstein, FBI agent," he said. "As you can see, I was under cover." Then he explained the menacing messages Josie had been receiving, and upon which the kidnapper had acted. He stepped over Richards' inert body and dragged it over to one of the kitchen chairs the other women had been tied to and set Richards on it. Andy reached around, picked up the strewn neckties, and gave Richards a taste of his own medicine. By the time he stood back to admire his handy work, they could hear sirens approaching.

"We're so grateful you're here," Mrs. Sloan finally spoke. "What I can't understand is why my husband didn't come looking for me sooner. I've been gone over 24 hours!"

"We might still be in the dark about your disappearance if you hadn't been with these other two ladies." Andy smiled. "You husband received a type-written note from you saying you'd gone to the spa because you'd had a rough week at work. He didn't even know you were missing."

"My word! Well, in that case, there was a silver lining around you two going missing."

"I'm just glad this guy wasn't any more dangerous than he was," Mrs. Garvey said.

"Right," Mrs. Coleson joined in. "He didn't have any other interest in us other than to keep us hostage, and now we know why."

Uniformed police officers entered the room, guns drawn. When they saw Richards tied up and the women free, they lowered their weapons.

"Which one of you is Andy Hoverstein? Or is Andy a guy's name?" the lead officer asked. "In which case, where is he?"

"I'm right here," Andy said, pulling off his wig with much effort. "I've been undercover."

Just then Richards came too and started moaning. Andy pulled the gag out of his mouth and said, "Had enough of your own medicine, Richards? I'm FBI Agent Andy Hoverstein, and I'm putting you under arrest."

Chapter Sixteen
That's My Collar!

"You have the right to remain silent, and a right to a lawyer," Andy told Richards, "but I'm guessing the more cooperative you are the easier this will go for you. Tell me, what is you beef with Josie Buchannon?"

Richards squeezed his eyes a couple of times, still trying to focus them. He looked up at the de-wigged police officer and nearly choked. He glared at Andy and said, "Josie got my job. I've been working in the mail room for over seven years. I applied for the accounting position when it came up. I even applied to go to California with the big-wigs, but of course, I didn't qualify. Josie got it all. She didn't need a bridal shower, too. She doesn't work for GS&A anymore!" Then he clammed up.

"Take him away, officers," Andy directed. "Be sure you finish Mirandizing him. No loop holes. And, remember, he's my collar."

The officers had called for a transport to take the hostages back to their precinct for questioning. When they were through, the women and Andy, who had wiped off most of his makeup, met up at the front desk where Mr. Coleson and P.J. had brought the rest of the bridal party. Mr. Sloan and Mrs. Garvey had also arrived to pick up their wives.

"What happened?" Josie asked Andy.

"Let's take this party into the conference room," the desk sergeant suggested. "Please follow me." He led the way down the hall and around the corner to a room not quite adequate for the gathering. The ladies took the chairs around the table and the men stood behind them. Andy strode to the head of the table and looked around at the crowd. The desk sergeant shut the door on his way out. Then Andy explained how he made the perfect bait to capture Richards.

"Once he took me back to his lair, I was able to make sure the women were all in one place and safe. I hadn't figured he'd fall for my costume, though, which played in my favor. In fact, I thought for sure he would have pulled off my wig before we even got there. I had to be ready for anything. Luckily, it worked."

Nods and comments of agreement rippled around the room.

"That about sums it up," Andy continued. "The kidnapper is in custody and the women have been returned to their husbands. I'm going to head home, and I recommend the Garveys and the Sloans do the same, since they live here. But perhaps the Colesons can put the rest of you up one more night. I don't recommend you driving after having been through so many traumas." He headed to the door, but couldn't leave until he had shaken hands with every male in the room and received a hug from every female.

"Thank you so much," Josie said, having waited until last to speak with Andy. "I can't thank you enough for coming to my rescue. Correction, our rescue." Josie hugged Andy. He squeezed her hard and quick and pushed her away.

"Now don't go making a habit of this!" he told her. "I might not be available the next time that you're in trouble. So, just don't get into any more trouble. Okay?"

"Okay, I'll try not to," she said and let him slip out the door.

The Sloans and the Garveys said good night to Josie and said they would see her at her wedding in a couple of months. Then Mr. Coleson got everyone's attention and said they should head back to his place. He and P.J. would drive the vehicles and divided up the bridesmaids. They headed out of the conference door.

Down the opposite way from the front door, another door opened and an officer was escorting Terry Richards, who was now in handcuffs. They paused and returned the gaze the bridal party gave them. Donna sprang out from behind Josie and Jes and ran up to Richards. She hauled back and smacked his face hard.

"You bastard!" she shouted and spat in his face. "And, here I trusted you! I let you take me to the New Year's Eve Ball! And, to think I almost slept with you! Go to hell!"

She whipped around and marched back to her friends.

"Are you going to let her get away with that?" Richard asked the officer. "Isn't that assault or something?"

"Or something," Josie heard the officer respond. "You want to press charges? Who's going to testify on your behalf? All I saw was a jilted girlfriend chew you out. That's very common, don't you think? What's not common is one guy kidnapping four women and taking them all to the same one-room apartment. If you'd have left them alone long enough, they would have untied each other. How stupid are you, anyway? Get moving."

"Come on, let's go," Mr. Coleson said and escorted his wife to the door. "There's nothing more to see here." Everyone else put on their coats and followed them out of the building and into the night. Josie crawled into P.J.'s car and belted herself in. Out the passenger door, Josie noticed Andy had stopped by the car to say a special goodbye to Vikki. Vikki was leaning into his space and gazing into his eyes.

"I'm glad you were safe the entire time," Andy said. "I didn't want any of you girls to get hurt."

"I'm glad you were on the job," Vikki purred. "I knew all along you would get your man. It was almost funny, though, what a cute Hildy you made."

"I hope she never sees a picture of me undercover as her. You won't give away too many details will you? I mean, after all, you shouldn't be discussing the case with anyone outside the operation until Richards has been tried and convicted."

"We'll get to talk again, won't we? You and me, that is. We'll have to go over our testimonies, won't we?"

"That is usually done with the state prosecutor, but I wouldn't mind seeing you again before the trial." Vikki was leading Andy. "In fact, why don't you come to Josie and P.J.'s wedding? It would be nice to see you under happier circumstances and not under cover!" They chuckled at her unintended pun. Andy helped Vikki into the back seat of the car behind Josie and shut the door. Vikki immediately opened the window.

"Put your seat belt on!" Andy reminded her and turned to leave.

"'Bye," Vikki cooed. Andy waived over his shoulder and kept walking.

P.J. drove with one arm around Josie all the way back to his parents' house. She was so relieved and happy to be back in his arms.

"I can't tell you how happy I am to have you here with me," Josie said, gazing up at her fiancé as he helped her out of his car. "But I have this nasty headache coming on. Do you think your parents would have something I could take for it?"

"I bet they do. Just go into the medicine cabinet in the bathroom and help yourself. I'll be in the living room channel surfing." He gave her a peck on the nose and headed off to find the remote.

"Good night, Josie! I'm headed off to the bed to catch some shut-eye!" Vikki said and gave Josie a hug. "Sleep tight!"

"Me, too!" Donna said and followed Vikki up the stairs.

Josie waived to their backs and went to the bathroom to take some headache medicine and found some sleep aid in the bathroom cabinet. She took two and went to find P.J. in the living room.

"Come here, you!" P.J. said. Reaching for her hand, he pulled her down, onto the sofa next to him and encased her in his arms. "There's not much on TV tonight, just a rerun of Sleepless in Seattle." "That's okay. I'm not really in the mood to watch television anyway." She yawned and then snuggled closer to P.J. He pulled the afghan from the back of the sofa and draped it over the both of them. When he turned his face to give Josie a good night kiss, she was already asleep. Not again, he thought with a smile. He managed to clap off the lights before kissing her forehead and drifted off to sleep himself. They slept like babies in each other's arms on the sofa, as had become their custom.

The Coleson house was buzzing like a honey farm the next morning. Mrs. Coleson was busy making breakfast in the kitchen. Mr. Coleson was helping her by setting the table and getting his family ready for church. The twins were talking at light speed to anyone who would listen.

"Hello, Grams?" Josie had decided to call her grandmother before church to let her know everything was back to normal and that she was feeling much better than she had last night.

"Why, hello, dear! I didn't expect to hear from you this morning. You weren't very talkative yesterday."

"No, and I was rather rude, too. I am so sorry! It's just that there was so much going on and I felt responsible for it all!"

"Nonsense, pussycat! I know you didn't do anything bad on purpose," Eleanor said soothingly. "Why don't you and P.J. come to supper tonight and tell me everything about your trip? Hmmm?"

"That sounds great, Grams! What can I bring?"

"Just yourself and P.J. I did some baking yesterday and put a pot roast in the slow cooker already. It'll be just fine. Tell P.J. 'hi' and to drive safely. See you tonight, say 5 p.m.?"

"Will do. See you then, Grams!"

After a hot breakfast and some mighty quick showers, the Colesons and their guests attended church, even Donna who claimed not to be very religious but seemed to participate as much as the next girl.

After lunch at Olive Garden, Josie asked Vikki to drive the Impala and take Jessica and Donna home while she rode with P.J. They let the girls head out first so they could say goodbye to the Colesons.

Later, back in Lakewood, Josie and P.J. headed over to the apartment building an hour early so they could visit with Eleanor without food in their mouths.

Chapter Seventeen
Home Again

"Have a seat kids," Eleanor pointed to the familiar kitchen set that had once been in her old Victorian home. They sat and looked at each other questioningly.

"You go ahead, Josie," P.J. conceded. "It's your story. I just went to New York City to try to rescue you again. This time, Andy got the collar." They both chuckled at that.

"Well, Grams, it's like this," Josie said and gave the account of all the menacing messages she had received from a stranger at the time of her first shower and following through to the one in New York City. "So, I called Andy Hoverstein and asked him to help. I even came up with the idea for him to go as Hildy, you know—undercover, since Hildy wasn't able to go."

"He even looked a lot like Hildy," P.J. interjected. "That was spooky!"

Josie went on to tell how the kidnappings unfolded and how the girls cowered at the Colesons, worrying about what happened to Andy and who was going to be next. "I kept the girls together as much as possible, telling them they couldn't even go to the bathroom alone!" They all rolled their eyes. "And, we called P.J. and Mr. Coleson, and they came right away."

"By the time we got there, even though we didn't know it, Andy. had already knocked out Richards and called the cops to come to his apartment. That's where Richards kept all three women."

Eleanor gasped at every turn in the story and clutched her blouse front as if to hang on tight to her heart. "What's going to happen now?"

"Andy's interrogating Terry Richards this afternoon. He said he would call when they're through. My phone should be ringing any time now," Josie said.

"It should be a slam-dunk case," P.J. added. "Andy and the three women were all held in Richard's apartment. Andy was there, too, as a hostage. All those eyewitnesses would be hard, if not impossible, to refute. The jury should eat up the fact that one of the 'girls' took down Richards after having been a hostage himself."

"Let's hope so," Eleanor said in agreement. "We don't want any loopholes that would allow that guy to duck the charges."

As if on cue, Josie's cellphone rang, "Our God is an Awesome God." She answered while P.J. and Eleanor looked on, listening.

"Uh huh," Josie said a couple of times. Then, "Thank you, Andy. We appreciate everything you've done to help us! Goodbye!"

Josie poked a 'Stop' command into her cellphone and put it back into her jeans pocket. She smoothed the front of her pink Argyle sweater and said, "Andy said there were probably absolutely no listening devices put into our vehicles, home or office. Although, I couldn't imaging that happening anyway merely because of how seldom we came into contact with him. I guess I was just being paranoid

"Andy also said Terry stated all his information came from Donna. He even stole my phone number out of her cellphone when she left it lay to go to the bathroom." Josie shook her head. "I feel sorry for her, for having been used like that!"

"That does beg the question as to how loyal she is to Sanderson and Sons, though," P.J. pointed out. "You'll have to interrogate her tomorrow!"

Monday morning arrived a lot sooner than Josie wanted it to. It took her by surprise when her alarm clock rang. It was still dark out, of course, being the dead of winter, in addition to the exhausting weekend. Josie had finished with her shower and decided to stand under a cold stream for as long as she could stand it, hoping it would wake her up.

She was alone in the house, now, and had to cook her own breakfast. This morning she made do with peanut butter toast and microwaved tea. She just didn't think it worth the bother to dirty a fry pan or two for just one person. When P.J. finally moved in, she would start making bigger breakfasts. Until then, something quick would do.

The drive to work was still dark and cloudy. Josie was grateful for automatic headlights because she would have been to drug out to remember to activate them. The same could be said for shutting them off once she reached the parking lot at work.

"Good morning, Josie!" Vikki sounded nearly as perky as always as she greeted her boss and best friend. Josie looked up to notice Vikki had slipped into a fitted red dress. *What an appropriate color for drab weather,* Josie thought. Aloud, she said, "Morning. What's new today?"

Vikki handed her a stack of messages indicating silently that Josie was late for work. She shook her head, but smiled a thank-you to Vikki and headed back to her office where she dumped everything on her desk and shed her wool coat. Punching up the intercom, she summoned Donna into her office. She hung her coat up and sat down behind her desk. This wasn't going to be pleasant, but it was necessary.

"Shut the door behind you, please," Josie said when Donna came in. "Please pull up a chair."

Donna complied and asked, "What's up, boss?"

"Unfortunately, you are," Josie said solemnly. "I need to ask you how much company information you divulged to Terry Richards. I need to know if your loyalty to Sanderson and Sons has deteriorated."

"No! I love this company! I love working here and would never jeopardize my job!" Donna shouted vehemently. "I can't imagine why you would even ask that! Just because I had a couple of dates with Terry when he was in town doesn't mean I sold out!"

"Okay. Okay. Say that I believe you, I still need to know what you told him so I can do damage control." Josie's gaze fixed on Donna's gem stone nose ring, pushing her black make-up to the fuzzy rear of Josie's vision.

"I only told him about the trip to New York City for the shower because he had asked me to go out that weekend. How did he get your phone number? It must have been when I invited him into my apartment to wait while I finished dressing. You know, it takes a long time to put all these earrings back in after having removed them to shower. He must have taken your phone number from my cellphone then, because it had been laying on the end table then. I didn't purposely tell him anything about work."

"Did he ever ask you anything about your job or where you worked, even just to be sociable?"

"No. I'd remember that after the ethics classes you made us take. I was very careful to keep our conversations to his racing, the weather or sex."

"Well, it's a good thing I have you all bonded, just in case he got any other information out of you, say maybe if you talk in your sleep? I don't want you to think I'm angry with you at this point. However, if I ever find out he did get more information than you want to admit to or have memory of giving him, I will have to fire you and recoup on the damages by applying for that bond to pay out. Am I making myself clear?"

"Yes, Ma'am!"

"Now, let's all get caught up on our work, okay? Scram!"

After Donna went back to her desk, Josie took the stack of messages Vikki had given her and started dialing. She had a lot of work to do before noon if she wanted to go to lunch with P.J. and work on their wedding plans. She also needed to do something about the fact that she still had not yet gotten a wedding gown!

Chapter Eighteen
Valentine's Day

Lunch with P.J. was rushed. Josie had an emergency meeting with a client promptly at 1 p.m.

"I'm sorry, P.J., but at least we solidified your groomsmen list and selected a formal wear store you can get them an appointment at for fitting," Josie apologized. She pulled a sky blue swatch out of her purse and handed it to him.

"What's this?" he asked, his eyes sparkled, reflecting the swatch's hue.

"This is a swatch of material from the bridesmaid's dresses. We need to find a tux that matches. How about if we go to Carol's Clothing Saturday morning and pick out the tux. You can give your groomsmen contact information to Carol at that time."

"Sounds good. What time?"

"Let's plan to leave about 9:45 as they open at 10 and close at noon. We could do lunch in that Oriental restaurant next to it, if that's okay."

"Sure. Then maybe we could go ice-skating. By the way, Saturday is Valentine's Day. Where would you like to go out to for supper?" He said, handing back the swatch. Then he paid the lunch tab as they walked out of the café.

"Ooh. The Fireside was nice for New Year's Eve. Could we go back there?"

"Yes, let's!" P.J. kissed her goodbye at her car and went around to his. "Oh, by the way! I found a buyer for my Cougar. My boss, Mr. Williams wants it. He's offered Blue Book pricing!"

"Whatever that is!" Josie laughed. "Sure. What do you plan to do with the money?"

"Give some, spend some and save some, like Dave Meyer preaches." They smiled across the top of his Chevy Cruise. Josie knew P.J. had received the Cougar for his 16th birthday and the electric blue Chevy Cruise as a college graduation present, both from his parents. The Cougar was becoming a "Classic", it was so old. "Mr. Williams collects old cars. You should see his collection sometime! See you Saturday!"

"'Bye!" Josie said and waived. She slid into Ruby, her Impala, and hurried back to the office. As she drove, she pulled out her cellphone and speed dialed a New York number.

"Sherrie's Shop! How can I help you?" the polite, but unfamiliar voice rang.

"This is Josie Buchannon. I'd like to speak with Sherrie, please."

"One moment, please, while I see if she's available."

"Thank you." Josie heard background music playing while she waited. It was the Theme to Ice Castles. Before it finished, though, the call was picked up.

"Josie! It's so good to hear from you! How can I help you?" Sherrie's voice enveloped Josie with a warm sense of friendship.

"I'm sorry I haven't called you sooner. I've been busy with a kidnapping case. But I'm getting married the first Saturday in April and I need a wedding dress! Can you help me?" Josie pleaded. "Please?"

"Of course, darling! I will make time for you. When can you come in for a fitting? Do Saturdays work best? How about this weekend?"

"I'm busy Saturday, with it being Valentine's Day and all. How about Sunday afternoon? Are you open Sunday's?"

"Not usually, so that actually makes it perfect! How about 2 o'clock?"

"Perfect! Wonderful! Thanks so much!"

"While we work, you must tell me about this kidnapping case!" Sherrie demanded.

"Certainly! I have to meet a client now and let you get back to work. See you Sunday!" Josie was able to relax a little and get to her appointment without feeling distracted with that major detail settled.

The rest of the week flew by and Valentine's Day had arrived. Josie woke with a sinus headache for which she took a couple of acetaminophen tablets that contained antihistamine and a steamy shower. *I feel like crawling back into bed,* she thought as the hot water ran down her back. *Come on, Josie! Put on your perky smile. P.J. will be here soon.* She crawled out of the shower and into her powder blue turtleneck and matching stretch pants. They would be comfortable for skating in later.

P.J. was prompt and escorted her to the car, putting her skates in the back seat for her, next to his.

"You're a little quiet this morning, hon. What's the matter?" he asked.

"I woke up with this sinus headache. The fresh air should help clear it up," she answered and pulled on her sunglasses. She laid the seat back down and rested all the way to the formal shop. P.J. politely kept quiet.

Inside Carol's Clothing, the attendant ushered them back to the formal wear department and showed them their catalog. She took P.J.'s measurements and brought him a white tuxedo to try on. With the headache, now dulled by medication, Josie dully sat on the high stool next to the catalog stand and limply held the dress swatch while she waited until P.J. came out of the dressing room. She smiled wanly as he pirouetted in front of her.

"You look dreamy, P.J.," she managed. "You'd look good in a potato sack, but I really like that tux on you, only I think it should have tails. And, white patent leather shoes, not navy socks." She winked to ease the dullness of her voice. P.J. just nodded and looked expectantly at the attendant. She smiled and nodded as well, and went in search of one with tails. She returned shortly with shoes as well. P.J. took them and went back into the changing room.

"Is that a swatch from your bridesmaid dresses?" the attendant asked. "Would you like to see some cummerbunds or tuxes in that shade of blue?" Josie nodded and tried to smile. *Some shopping trip! I can't even enjoy it fully,* Josie thought. *Oh, well, this should clear up once we're out skating.*

P.J. came out dressed as he would on his wedding day and Josie was very pleased with the picture. They quickly picked out matching groomsmen tuxes and decided to use them for the ushers as well. P.J. gave his friends' contact information to the attendant and took Josie out to lunch.

Josie ended up eating the egg drop soup and not much else, but P.J. savored three plates full of various dishes, plus dessert.

"It's a good thing we're going skating," she said, poking P.J. in the belly on their way back to the car. "You can wear off all that food you ate!" They both laughed. She took a long, cleansing breath of fresh air before crawling into the car.

"Feeling better?" P.J. asked her.

"Some," she said. "I know it will clear up once we've been skating a while. Fresh winter air helps tame the inflammation in my sinuses." Soon, she was proven right. They enjoyed the rest of the afternoon and went back to her house to change for supper.

The Fireside Inn was just as cozy and romantic as it had been on New Year's Eve. Josie and P.J. exchanged Valentine cards while they ate ribeyes and salads. Josie gave P.J. a wedding cross pendant to wear on their wedding day. P.J. presented Josie with the ruby heart pendant she had been dreaming of.

"Pick you up for church tomorrow?" P.J. asked as he was kissing her goodnight.

"Yes, if you want to go to the 8:30 a.m. service," she answered nodding. "I have a dress fitting at 2 o'clock in New York and want to have an early lunch."

"No problem," P.J. said. "Did you want me to drive you?"

"Ha ha! Very funny!" Josie pushed lightly on his chest. "You know the tradition about the groom not seeing his bride in her wedding gown until she comes down the aisle. It's bad luck if you do. No. I'm taking Vikki and Grams, of course. I just hope the roads aren't too icy."

"Tomorrow should be fine, but if we continue to drive back and forth, like to holidays with my family, we should get one of those SUVs everyone's so crazy about."

"That would probably be a smart thing to do," Josie said.

"Okay, so that's what I'll do tomorrow afternoon while you're away. I'll go on the Internet and start the search."

With that decided, he gave her one last peck and left.

After church and brunch with Grams and Vikki, the next day, the threesome headed south to the big city. Josie was floating on a cloud as she drove and visited with her best friend and grandmother. Her heart was filled with love for all and she radiated with the bridal bliss that she had only read about until she met P.J.

Finally they arrived at Sherrie's Shop where they were given the royal treatment. Vikki flitted about the store like a bumble bee bent on kissing every flower in the field. Grams was given a throne-like chair near the three-way mirror so she could watch Josie as she tried on several styles of gowns Sherrie had sewn in her off hours for display models.

"That one looks great on you," Sherrie would say each time Josie came out of the dressing room. "I like how the neckline lays on this one." Or, "That skirt looks great with your height." Once, she said, "You could use a little more bust, dear. That strapless dress just isn't going to stay up. You'll be flashing everyone besides P.J.!

"Here, I saved this one for last. I really think this is the one. No one else has had a chance to order this one," Sherrie said. "I designed it just for you." She handed Josie an opaque garment bag. Neither Josie nor her guests could see into it. Josie shrugged and took it into the dressing room. Sherrie came as well to help her change. "I had your measurements from that suit I made for you last summer and used them, with some additional seam allowance just in case you gained any weight over the fall and winter."

Josie nodded and smiled. She unzipped the garment bag, which Sherrie whisked away, revealing the most exquisite gown Josie had ever seen. Her eyes grew as large as saucers and her mouth fell open in awe. For a moment she just stood there gazing at it, drinking it in with her eyes. When she couldn't take it anymore, Sherrie took the hanger from Josie and slid it onto the hook on the wall.

"Let's get you out of this other dress and into that one, okay, honey?" Sherrie began to unzip the gown Josie was in and to slide it down to the floor. Josie stepped out of it as if she was in a daze. She stood there in her bikini panties and the strapless, long-line bra Sherrie had provided for the fitting. Gingerly, she reached out her hand and gently stroked the lacey neckline of the gown hanging on the hook. Sherrie reached up as well and drew the dress off the hanger, undid the zipper in the back and rolled up the hem to meet the armpits so Josie could slide into it like a little child getting help dressing from his mother. Once the zipper was secured; Josie whirled to face the mirror.

The effect was transforming. A mock turtleneck made of Victorian lace, which matched the lace that covered the bodice and barely covered the décolleté, caressed Josie's neck. The sleeves were made of the same sheer lace, with ruffles at the cuff. The A-line skirt dusted the floor with a flounce. The underskirt was chalk white. Josie stared at herself in the mirror.

Sherrie reached into the garment bag and pulled out a white beaded Juliet cap with a full-length veil. The sides of which were also trimmed in the Victorian lace. She placed it on Josie's head as if she were crowning her Homecoming

Queen. Josie was transfixed to the point that Sherrie had to practically drag her away from the mirror.

"Come on, honey. Your grandmother and maid of honor want to see you in that dress."

Sherrie escorted Josie to the mirror area and handed her up onto the dais, then began to straighten the flowing veil behind Josie. Josie gazed into the three-way mirror and turned ever so slowly as to admire every angle of the gorgeous gown she was ecstatic to be wearing. Not only was it beautiful, but it fit her like a glove. Sherrie was a genius! This was the gown.

As she turned further to ask her grandmother what she thought of the dress, she didn't have to say a word. It was written on her grandmother's face; tears of joy rolled down her cheeks. Eleanor's eyes sparkled with their wetness and her face was lit by the brightest smile Josie could remember ever having seen. Her hands clasped in mid-air.

Josie turned to Vikki for her reaction. Vikki was speechless. Her eyes wide and her mouth hung open. Then she broke her pose and exploded into a cheer. "Woo hoo! Is that for you! Or, what! That's the one!"

"You think so?" Josie managed. Both Eleanor and Vikki nodded emphatically.

Sherrie gently touched Josie on the forearm to get her attention. "Like I said, I left plenty of seam allowance, if you find you need tailoring closer to the wedding. Just call me if you need to set that second appointment. Plus, I'll alter your bridesmaids' dresses for them at a 20 percent discount."

Josie snapped out of her daze, turned toward Sherrie and asked, "How much for this dress?"

"What do you care, girl? You're rich, you can afford it!" Vikki shouted.

"How much?" Josie asked again, ignoring Vikki."

"I'm giving it to you for cost," "Sherrie said. "The labor is my wedding gift to you. The cost of the material is $500.00."

"And, I'll pay that," Eleanor interjected, fishing in her purse for her checkbook.

"No, Grams. You don't have to. I can well afford to pay for my own dress. Besides, you already gave me the house as a wedding present."

"Nonsense, Josie girl," her grandmother argued. "As your parent figured, it is my loving duty to help pay for your wedding. You have already paid for most of it. Please let me just get the dress for you. It would make me so very happy."

"Listen to your grandmother, Josie," Vikki said. "Be a little traditional, to go along with that beautiful dress!"

Josie looked from her grandmother to Vikki and back to Grams. Then she shrugged in defeat. "If you say so, Grams. I do want to make you happy."

"Great! Let's get you out of this dress, Josie, and I'll box it up for you," Sherrie said, tugging on Josie's elbow.

The dress was the last major item on Josie's wedding list. She was very pleased to have that all wrapped up. The trip back to Lakewood was chaotic, with all three women chatting up a storm.

Before they knew it, St. Patrick's Day had whizzed by, and they were counting down the days until the big weekend. Josie had put notices up on all the social media that the agency would be closed that Friday in preparation for the Groom's Supper that night and the wedding the next day.

Nearly 300 guests had responded to the ornate wedding invitations that had been mailed out a month before. They were all excited about seeing Josie and P.J. get married.

That Friday, Josie and her bridal party went to the local salon for a pre-trial on wedding hairstyles. They would make another visit the next morning to freshen them up for the ceremony. After the salon, they made a trip to St. Andrew's to hang up their dresses and let them breath. The florist would be delivering the bouquets and the altar flowers the next morning. The caterer said they would deliver the cake by noon, just hours prior to the ceremony. The photographer said she would arrive an hour before the ceremony to take some informal shots, but promised to save the combination pictures until after the ceremony, per Josie's instructions. Everything was falling into place.

Josie decided to wear the navy suit from Sherrie for the groom's supper. She didn't see the need for a new outfit. She felt she had spent plenty of money already on the wedding. Besides, the suit was dressy and deserved to be worn more than she had done. P.J. also wore his navy suit and picked up Josie 20 minutes before they had to be at the church for the dinner. He presented her with a red rose corsage as she opened the door to greet him.

"Oh, thanks, P.J.! That was very thoughtful of you," Josie said, and opened the container for him to pin it on her. And, they were on their way.

P.J.'s parents had hired the same caterer as was serving the wedding for the groom's supper. They had selected a menu of a double roast, pork and beef, with mashed potatoes and gravy, sweet corn and ice cream sundaes for dessert. When everyone was nearly finished eating, the best man stood for his toast.

"I know the big toasts are saved for the wedding dinner, but I had some informal things I wanted to say to P.J. and Josie," Stan said as he lifted his wine glass. "P.J. has been my best friend ever since we were in school together. I love you, buddy! I've known him to date a lot of girls, but most of them weren't serious in any fashion. He was previously engaged once, but, Josie, I want you to know nothing happened between him and Pricilla. This man is still as pure as the driven snow. I don't know how he lasted this long, especially after meeting you, but we have to give him credit. He's a saint. The way he talks about you, I would think he would have made a move on you already, but he says he hasn't. I have to believe that. So, here's to a match that really must have been made in heaven! Cheers!"

"That was a little too personal," P.J. whispered to Stan as he sat down. "Please don't say any of that tomorrow." Stan just grinned at him in response.

"Huh hmm," Vikki cleared her throat as she stood. "I guess that means I should practice, too. I, too, have known Josie all my life and am blessed to call her my BFF. I don't have any intimate stories to tell. Josie would shoot me if I did, right Josie? Anyway, I know the two of them will be happy together; they were made for each other. And, I ask God to bless their marriage with strength, unity and love all their days. Everybody say, 'Amen'!"

"Amen!" the gathering chorused. Vikki sat down. P.J. and Josie stood.

"I want to thank you all for coming and participating in our wedding events tonight and tomorrow," P.J. said. "You all are a very special part of our lives and, even if someone got a little too personal, we love you all. Thanks!"

"I'll second that," Josie said. "We love you and wouldn't want to do this without your blessings. So, thank you." They sat, and soon people were coming up to their table to wish them well before leaving for the evening.

Soon, Josie and P.J. were able to leave as well. Josie lingered by the front door of her home to say goodnight to

P.J. She kissed him deeply and said, "You go home, now. You're not coming in and sleeping on my couch the night before our wedding."

P.J. moaned playfully, but obeyed. He drove away in anticipation of the following night when neither one would have to get up and go home.

Chapter Nineteen
White Wedding

Josie had gone upstairs alone. It was the night before her wedding and so much excitement had preceded it, she didn't think she'd have much trouble sleeping, but she took a couple of sleep aid as a precaution. Even then, she tossed and turned half the night before falling asleep. Her dreams were fraught with frustration. She dreamed she had trouble getting out of bed in the morning, her legs were solid cement, but in reality just caught up in the covers. When she finally extricated herself and was able to get into the shower, there wasn't any hot water. The icy water that rained on her head made her scream. Her make-up turned out like Donna's Gothic look, and her wedding dress, which she dreamed was at home for her to put on, ended up getting caught in the door of the car and tearing. She couldn't imagine what else could go wrong until she had gone through the march and gotten to the altar. There, waiting for her in the maid of honor position, was her arch nemesis, Cass! Josie screamed so loudly, she woke herself up.

Thank God I'm alone in the house, Josie thought. If Grams were still here, she would have had a heart attack! And, praise God my legs are fine! Hopefully, the shower is hot. Josie hurried through her morning ablutions and was having breakfast when her cellphone rang.

"Good morning, dear!" Grams' voice came across to her. "How are you this morning?"

"I had a nightmare about this morning, but I'm okay. How about you?"

"Doing well and will be coming over to the church around 1 o'clock as you suggested. Sid will be picking me up, just like last night. I just wanted to know if there was anything you needed. You know, 'Something old, something new, something borrowed, something blue'? I have an old handkerchief of your great grandmother's, if you like you may borrow it. It even has some blue embroidery on it. You could carry it under your bouquet. And, it would serve as something borrowed as well as something old and something blue!"

"Perfect, Grams! I love you! Please bring it along. Something new would be my dress, of course, and the hanky takes care of the rest. Fabulous! See you there!" Josie finished up breakfast and left for the church. She had given P.J. specific instructions about which door he and his groomsmen were to enter the church to avoid seeing his bride before the ceremony.

Josie drove slowly and carefully, as there was new-fallen snow on the ground. She wondered what Grams' would say about that. Eleanor always had an old wives' tale or an anecdote about everything. If it rained on your wedding, you would be rich. If the sun shone, you'd be happy. Well, today's forecast was for a sunny afternoon. However, Gram's predictions didn't really cover snow.

Just then her cellphone rang again. It was Grams' again.

"I forgot to mention: I've had to do some research on this, but I found that if it snows on your wedding day, your life will be full of adventure!"

"Now, how did you know? I was just thinking about those old sayings!" They laughed together and hung up. The phone rang again.

"Hello, my bride!" P.J.'s voice came over the phone, pumping adrenaline into Josie's system.

"Hello, P.J." she answered. "What's up? Is something wrong?"

"No," he said. "I just wanted to wish my best girl a happy wedding day! You said I couldn't see you before the ceremony. You didn't say I couldn't talk to you!"

"You got me there!" Josie was secretly pleased he found a way around her restrictions.

"Hey, hon, I know the road could be a little slippery, with all the new snow and all, so I'll let you go. I just wanted to hear your voice before we meet at the altar. I love you!"

"I love you, too, P.J. 'Bye!"

At the church, Vikki saw her arrive and ran out to meet Josie. She gave her a big hug and said, "This is it! You're getting married!" She squealed in Josie's ear. "Now, let's get you inside!" They rushed in through the side door that led directly to the Ladies Room, on the opposite side of the church basement from the Men's Room.

The other girls, along with Grams, were there to start getting ready for the wedding. Dresses started flying and makeup brushes feathered face powder into the air.

Grams pressed her mother's handkerchief into Josie's hand and gave her a hug. "God bless your marriage, dear. I'm so proud of you."

"I love you, too Grams. Thanks! Now get upstairs for your picture!" Then Eleanor left to find Sid and wait for her cue to enter the church.

Finally, with Hildy's help, Josie was ready to go to the stairs and wait for the Bridal March. When Hildy lowered the veil over Josie's face, Josie's eyes inspected the other woman's outfit. Hildy had found a sky blue pantsuit and paired it with a navy blue silk top. She wore navy pumps to match. Josie was surprised to see the production specialist in heels and said so.

"Your suit is fabulous," she told her personal attendant, "but, I'm surprised to see you wearing heels."

"Well, they're chunky and low enough they aren't too uncomfortable. Anyway, you are the center of attention, Josie. That fitted gown clings to you in all the right places. Wow!" Hildy said. Then she turned to the rest of the bridesmaids and said, "Okay, girls, get lined up now!"

Josie mused at how readily Hildy had taken to her role in the wedding. She seemed to enjoy telling the others what to do, where to stand, and how to fix their dresses.

Soon the organ was playing Jesu Son of Man's Desiring, aka Joy and Patti led the procession down the aisle. When she had taken two steps down, Pauline fell in line, and so forth until all the bridesmaids had met up with their escorts and released them to find their designated spots.

Then the organ began playing the Bridal March, and Dana Garvey met Josie. He gave her a hug and wished her good luck. She took his arm and they proceeded down the aisle toward P.J. Josie was grateful to have an arm to lean on. She was feeling a little lightheaded because of all the high drama of being the center of attention in such an elegant affair. She looked straight ahead at Rev. Van Mevren and took a couple of deep breaths to calm her giddiness.

P.J. took her hand from Mr. Garvey's. Only then did Josie look at P.J. His eyes twinkled and his smile radiated his happiness. Josie relaxed. She knew, without a doubt, they both wanted this; they both wanted to be married forever.

As they exchanged vows, Josie's heart drummed her love for P.J. so loudly; she would have sworn he could hear it too. He squeezed her hand almost as if he could read her mind.

"I promise to love, honor, and cherish you for the rest of our life together," Josie repeated after the minister. Pride swelled her heart and it nearly burst as she heard P.J. say the same words. Tears welled in her eyes.

Rev. Van Mevren pronounced the blessing. Then Bobbi sang her solos, God a Woman and a Man accompanied the lighting of the unity candle, and then The Lord's Prayer. The ceremony went so fast, Josie was in a daze. Soon, Reverend Van Mevren was introducing Mr. and Mrs. Paul Coleson, Jr. Then Amy was playing the Trumpet Fanfare, which was the recessional, and Josie and P.J. were in the receiving line, hugging and shaking hands with an endless number of well-wishers.

The reception and dance went off as planned. After the grand march to Have I Told You Lately (That I Love You), Josie and P.J. were split up most of the evening, dancing to the tunes of the Happy Wanderers. Finally, Stan rounded them up for the Dollar Dance, which came as a surprise to Josie, but she danced until her feet were tire.

Then during a band break, Stan and Vikki sat Josie on a chair and lifted her dress to her knee to show off the garter belt. Stan started taking bids on it. Josie quickly slid the baby blue garment from her leg and dropped her skirt to cover up again. She slid the garter over Stan's pointing hand and walked off the floor. He could have the thing if he wanted it, but she wasn't going to expose herself to model it.

Coming up behind her, P.J. put his arm around her and whispered in her ear. "I'm sorry about that, Josie. I didn't realize Stan was planning to do that. Do you want me to tell him off for you?"

"No," Josie said, shaking her head. "Don't make a scene. The dance is almost over."

Just then Vikki came up and took Josie by the arm. In her other hand, she carried Josie's throwaway bouquet. "Please come throw your bouquet, now, Josie! I've gotten the bridesmaids together, except for Jes, of course. The bandleader is going to announce the bouquet toss and invite all the single women to the front to try to catch it!"

Josie gave P.J. a quick peck and followed her maid of honor out onto the floor.

"Can we have the bride come up on stage?" the bandleader was saying. Josie went up the side steps and onto the stage to stand next to him. He turned her around and said, "Just stand there until I count to three, okay?" Into the microphone, he said, "All single ladies, ready to catch the bouquet? Remember, the one who catches it will be the next one to get married! Here we go! One, two, three!"

Josie hefted the bouquet backwards over her head and whirled around just in time to see Hildy catch it. Josie chuckled to herself. She didn't even know if Hildy was seeing anyone. Then she spotted Vikki, whose bottom lip hung out and her eyes were brooding as she pouted over not being the one to catch the bouquet. *I bet Andy's relieved,* Josie thought. *He probably likes Vikki, but with his job, he won't be ready to settle down just yet.*

P.J. appeared at the foot of the stage and offered his arms to help Josie down from there. She leaned over and he whisked her away in his arms, her flowing white skirt fluttering with the movement.

"I'm ready to carry you over the threshold, Mrs. Coleson. Are you ready to be taken away from here?" P.J. asked her before setting her down.

"Yes! I thought you'd never ask! Just let me collect my veil, purse and coat," which she did so speedily that Vikki asked her if she was ill and had to leave before she threw up.

"No, you airhead!" Donna said, coming up behind her. "They're off to their honeymoon! And, not just for the travel, if you know what I mean!"

"Oh, Josie! You're going to find out just how beautiful it is to be with your husband!" Jessica said, her arms reached in to give Josie a hug.

"Leaving already?" Hildy asked. "Does that mean everyone has to leave? I danced with a cousin of P.J.'s that I'd like to get to know better." She waived the bouquet she caught, then sniffed it. "Hmm. Not real, but still smells nice!"

"You go right ahead and keep dancing," Josie said. "The band is supposed to keep playing until 1 o'clock. Don't let them stop a minute before that. Just P.J. and I are leaving for our honeymoon." She blushed at the thought of them alone together and for the first time not having to refrain from acting on their feelings.

"Goodbye!" "Good luck!" "God bless!" They left to cheers and hugs. Josie made sure she said goodbye to Eleanor and Sid. Her grandmother kissed them both, and Sid hugged Josie and shook hands with P.J.

The bridal couple didn't say a word on the drive back to the house they would now be sharing. Josie stayed in the car until P.J. came around and held open her door. After he closed it behind her, he swooped her up in his arms and carried her up the slippery sidewalk and over the threshold, just as he had promised. He leaned back on the door after closing it and kissed her long and passionately.

"Mmphf. P.J., I have to take my coat off, I'm getting overheated!" Josie said. It wasn't the romantic declaration he had been waiting for, but P.J. set her on her feet and helped her take off her long winter coat and hung it up in the closet for her. When he turned back to her, she had set down her purse and veil and was facing him as well. She reached up with both hands and slid her hands under the lapels of his tux jacket to remove it. The jacket slid to the floor where it stayed as P.J. pulled Josie into his embrace for another long, passionate kiss. Their pulses soared together. Time seemed to stand still.

"Lock the door, please, P.J.," Josie whispered with her eyes closed. As P.J. turned to do so, Josie slipped out of her wedding shoes and padded silently toward the steps. She halted with her back toward the door. "A little help, sir, if you please."

P.J. stepped out of his patent leather loafers and moved to unzip Josie's wedding dress. She let it fall at her feet and fled up the stairs to the master bedroom where a new king size bedroom set had been delivered two days prior. Josie had made it with brand new bedding and had fragranced the room with fresh flowers.

Stripping off his shirt, P.J. followed her. He stopped in the doorway and marveled at the sight. Josie was lighting candles in her lacey underwear. His eyes widened and a smile grew on his face. It broadened further when he watched as she slid between the crisp white sheets and moved over to make a place for him. That was his cue to strip off his t-shirt, which he threw back over his head into the hall. He closed the bedroom door behind him and unbuckled his belt as he moved closer to the bed. Dropping his pants and socks, he lay down in bed as Josie held up the bedclothes. She lowered them, put her arms around P.J.'s neck, and kissed him, their tongues danced together and their bodies pressed against each other. P.J. let his hands roam, gliding along the contours of Josie's back and buttocks. He felt her firm breasts peak through the thin film of her strapless bra against his chest. He drew her leg over his and moaned.

"I love you, P.J." Josie whispered in his ear. "I want you now." She stuck her tongue in his ear which she knew drove him wild. He groaned and rolled on top of her and kissed her hard, displaying more passion than she thought possible. She moaned, and he let up.

"I love you, too, Josie," P.J. responded. "Are you as ready as I am for you to be my wife?"

"Yes," she moaned again. They gave in to the passion they had been fighting for months, and consummated their marriage.

Chapter Twenty
Honeymoon Harmonics

Josie was sore the next morning, and took a long soak in the tub until P.J. threatened to join her. Then she hustled to get breakfast on the table.

"Thank you for coming back here to share our first night together as husband and wife," Josie said as they ate waffles and sausage links. "I can't tell you how much it meant to me."

"It's okay," P.J. said. "I actually agree: the first night should be in our own bed." Switching gears, he added, "Say, hon? On our way home from our honeymoon, how about stopping by a couple of car dealers? I found a couple of SUVs to look at."

"You want to talk cars when we have a honeymoon to look forward to? What a man!" Josie shook her head, but then leaned over and kissed her new husband on the cheek. She twirled her finger in the blond hair of his chest and started breathing heavily. The couple had come down to breakfast in their wedding underwear. P.J. noticed her heavy breathing and was watching her lacey bra move in and out seductively. He leaned down to possess her mouth and reached out to stop the movement he had been witnessing.

"Mmm. Do I get breakfast like this every day?" P.J. asked, coming up for a breather.

"No," Josie said, pushing him away. "I mean, I'd like to, but we'd never make it to work. And, since we have a whole week to make love, why don't you go shower while I take care of the dishes? We don't want to miss our flight to Kentucky."

P.J. whined and tried playfully to hang onto her as he stood up; she slid down his chest and rubbed against his body without meaning to. Josie felt electricity charge her own senses and nearly lost control, but swung away from him easily enough and wobbled toward the sink. P.J. came up behind her and gave her a bear hug.

"I love you! Why do you have to be so darned irresistible?" They laughed, and he gave her a kiss on the neck before heading off to the back stairs. "And, so responsible!" he flung over his shoulder.

< * >

After a week riding horseback and making love, Josie was saddle sore and spent a lot of time in the hot tub of their hotel suite. *I may be sore*, she thought, *but I couldn't be happier.*

Epilogue
One Year Later

P.J. and Josie were on their way to New York City to celebrate their one year wedding anniversary with his family. P.J. was behind the wheel of their black Chevy Trail Blazer. Josie was sitting in the back seat next to an infant car seat. She was cooing at their one-month-old baby, who was bundled in a pink snowsuit. Suddenly, the blazer hit a patch of ice and went into a tailspin. Fortunately, there were no other vehicles on the road at the moment, and P.J. expertly turned into the spin and regained control.

"I sure do love this four-wheel drive vehicle. Don't you, honey?" P.J. asked.

"Yes, you're right," Josie said, nodding and stroking baby Eleanor's face to soothe the frightened infant. "I no longer feel on the cutting edge of danger with you driving a vehicle that's on the cutting edge of technology."

Other Books by J.J. Luepke:

On the Cutting Edge: Redemption, Trafford Publishing,
© 2010
On the Cutting Edge: Retribution, Trafford Publishing,
© 2012
Rich By Accident, CreateSpace, © 2012